# The Chronicles of David King
## Lost & Found

*Jonathan E. Lambe I*

# The Chronicles of David King
## Lost & Found

*Jonathan E. Lambe I*

**X3 MEDIA GROUP**
Pembroke, Bermuda

*The Chronicles of David King — Lost & Found*
Published by:
X3 Media Group
6 Deep Dale Rd
Pembroke, HM18
Bermuda
www.DKNovel.com
1-800-609-4907
1-862-367-0032
ISBN 978-0-9857081-0-8

Book production by:
Silver Lining Creative
A Division of Pivot Point Publishing
www.SilverLiningCreative.com

Edited by Tammy Leigh Maxey

Printed in the United States of America.

# Dedication

I would like to dedicate this book to those that are on, or just beginning, your journey of discovering and pursuing greatness. You were designed to rule and reign in life, to have dominion — not be dominated by situations, circumstances, people or substances. I am proud of you and excited that, just like David, you too will rise above the cards you were dealt in life — other people's ideas and agendas for you - and you will discover the king — the ruler — the cultural architect God has purposed you to be. Join the movement: 10XBC = 10 Times Better than the Culture!

# Special Thanks

I would like to thank my "support system" for being there throughout this journey — I could not have done this without your love, patience, and encouragement:

- To Cheryl "Binky" Bias for always keeping me focused — and out of jail (lol).

- To Pastor Chyanna Mull-Anthony for lending a listening ear and encouraging me to keep going.

- To Latisha Lister for helping me to think more like an author than a movie producer.

- To all the youth pastors that read the manuscript and gave great feedback.

- To Dave Sawler for giving me the heads up on the process of authoring a book.

- To Deaven and Linda Butler, Tammy Maxey, and the entire Pivot Point Publishing family — you all are simple amazing!

- To Akili Richards, the greatest artist I know. You are a legend and you are destined to leave a great legacy.

- To Pastor Jamie Jeter Massey for taking the time out of your busy schedule to share in this project and write the foreword to this book. I have no words to adequately express my appreciation — Thank You!

- To everyone who listened and said, "You can do it."

- To my parents, Pastors Harold and Marilyn Lambe who supported the project before they knew what they were getting into.

- To my sister Joy, for all your creativity (that drives me nuts sometimes), thank you for your involvement and contribution.

- To Aunt Millicent Mills for always encouraging me and supporting me without ever asking for anything in return — you are truly amazing!

- To my magnificent wife, Candice Renee Spann Willis Lambe, you are my rock, my heart, and the air I breathe. Your contribution has been priceless.

# Contents

# Preface

I am amazed and in awe to see the completed product of my first novel — if only my English teachers could see me now! I was the student that made most teachers shake their head in pity. I was likable but disorganized, the class clown, a dreamer. I learned how to cram enough information to pass my exams, but never retained the information. I had a severe fear of failure. I never felt as if I was good enough at anything, so I chose not to study or try hard, opting instead to receive average scores with the fallback excuse, "I did fairly well for not studying."

I always had an excuse, something or someone I could blame, so I did not have to rise to my potential. I read somewhere (and I am paraphrasing) that if you do not decide to become great, by default you have decided to practice mediocrity. I found out that my greatness was not in my abilities, talents, or gifts, but it was to be found in the one that created me and you — God Himself. Because of His greatness, greatness is embedded into our DNA! It is our job to believe it, discover it, and pursue it by taking the limits off. There are many enemies combating us in our own greatness and destiny — they may be generational, economical or spiritual, a sense of poor self-worth, abuses... the list goes on and on. However, one thing I do know is that God has given us everything we need to overcome and conquer every enemy we may face. So, as you read this ancient story with a modern twist, I pray that you are entertained but also inspired, challenged, and empowered to see yourself and rise above every giant in your life. To walk in the greatness that is already in you.

I wrote this novel as authentically as I could without trying to offend, but life is complex and chaotic, and many are dealing with things that our culture does not like to talk about. The Bible is unapologetically bold on issues many of a "softer society" find distasteful, but it is real. So if there are areas of offense, please be gracious and forgive, as my heart is to inspire those who are in the trenches of a drama-filled life with no light in sight. King David lived a life that was often unpleasant, dramatic, and at times even dark, but he was truly a man after God's own heart. There is hope on the other side. So I pray you enjoy this first book in the series inspired by his story with a fun, modern twist — *The Chronicles of David King: Lost & Found.*

# Foreword

Ifirst met Jonathan Lambe when I traveled to Bermuda to speak at a conference. As I entered the building, I heard soulful organ music playing that immediately grabbed my attention. There, perched on the organ stool was Jonathan playing with exceptional skill. I said to myself, "Now there is a talented young man!" I have since discovered just how multi-talented and diverse his artistic ability is.

In his book, *The Chronicles of David King*, Jonathan weaves in allegory form a modern day story of a biblical king that is sure to entice readers of every age. However, his unique perspective is certain to capture a younger audience that will relate to the life and challenges of its characters. With the same harmonious rhythm and flow that comes through in his music, Jonathan will draw you in and leave you anticipating more. You will be inspired and moved as you read about the life of David King.

— *Jamie Massey*

# Chapter 1
# Why Me?

David King's eyes were glued to the flashing big screen TV, his body almost numb with shock, as a local Orange County Community News reporter announced the latest crisis:

"Breaking news, Goliath holds Luas Corp hostage! What started out as a summer employment orientation has turned into a nightmare as hundreds of students are being held hostage by what seems to be a computer virus called 'Goliath.' A video message was broadcast during Mr. Luas' opening remarks to the new summer workers. This same video message was sent to our OCC News studio as well. The message claims that unless Luas Corp wires one billion dollars to a specified off shore account, the virus will be released. If that happens, it will destroy valuable company information, resulting in the complete demise of Luas Corp, not to mention the company's thousands of global employees that would suddenly be out of work. Any attempts to leave the building will be detected by booby-traps set throughout the facility, and the company's computers will simultaneously explode with the threat of fatal results. The virus is said to be released in just two hours."

David snatched up his cell phone and, with trembling fingers, frantically pounded the keypad, "Hello…hello…Mr. Luas?!"

A gruff and panicked voice squawked through the receiver, "Who is this? You'll never get away with this! You no good, son of a…"

"Mr. Luas, it's me, David!"

"David?" Mr. Luas shot back, his confusion obvious.

"David King, sir."

"Oh. I'm sorry son. For a minute there, I thought you might be the hacker.

This idiot is trying to extort a billion dollars from me!"

"I know. I saw the news, sir. But I can stop him."

"How? They have all the computers here at the office wired to explode if we so much as touch them, and they have already fried all the computers on the first floor. None of my IT guys know what to do. Besides that, nobody can leave! If anyone even tries..."

"What was that?" David nearly dropped the phone as the deafening noise shot through the receiver. "Mr. Luas, are you okay? Are you still there, are you alright? Mr. Luas? Hello?"

"I'm here. All the computers just went on the second floor!"

"Sir, listen to me. I can stop this guy. But I am going to need access to your personal code and password for the mainframe, and your private entrance at the club. Do you remember my first day working for you?"

"David, you are either brilliant or you are about to kill my company and send this town into an epic recession. Either way, we are depending on you, son. Here is my code…"

David closed his eyes to memorize the info, and suddenly it felt as if the world was moving in slow motion although his mind was racing.

Thinking aloud, David mused, "Who would have ever imagined when I started with this company just under a year-and-a-half ago that I would be here, with the fate of the city, and the livelihood of people worldwide, resting on my shoulders? Wow, things have certainly changed."

*18 months earlier...*

The dinner table felt cold despite the hot meal as the King family sat eating in silence. It was the first time David had ever dined with his father and new family.

Young David was the result of a love affair that Mr. King had just over seventeen years prior. Mr. King never knew about the son that resulted from the affair, not until about a month ago, that is, when he received an urgent call at his office from David's mother. Her hesitation was evident in her voice, and in the apologies she immediately offered, when he answered the phone. She did not wish to intrude on him after all these years, but she had no choice. She was dying. Breast cancer was the culprit, and it was rapidly staking its claim. Time was running out for her to make her peace with God and man, thus the phone call. She cried and begged his forgiveness for keeping his son a secret from him all those years. Even now, she regretted forcing the news on him this way, but she had no other family, and she did not know what else to do. She asked Mr. King to please take their son in and show him a 'good life.' Mr. King, a good and decent family man, agreed. A month later, David's mother passed away.

When David arrived at the King's home, he was a skinny sixteen-year-old kid still sporting a baby face. The Kings had rushed to at least provide the minimal pro-visions for David.

Two years ago, Mr. King had started to renovate the basement with his sons as a family project. However, the boys had soon found 'better things to do,' so the project continued to lay dormant. The basement looked like an unkempt construction site with tools and building materials scattered in a chaotic mess about the room. The Kings managed to set aside a small space for David equipped with a twin size bed and heater so he could at least be warm and comfortable. The basement was quite large and full of potential, large enough, in fact, to convert into a spacious two-bedroom apartment with its own outside entry. David did not complain. It was a place to lay his head, and much larger than anything he was use to.

After dinner that evening, David went straight to bed, but he couldn't sleep. As he lay in bed staring at the unfinished ceiling, he thought about his mother. He missed her so much! He ignored the hot tear that trickled down his face and disappeared into his pillow. He swallowed against the painful knot forming in his throat as he whispered, "God why are you doing this to me?" His body shuddered with emotion, and in the dark silence, David cried himself to sleep.

———◦◆◦———

The next morning David was startled awake by an angry argument that seemed to be escalating upstairs.

"Why does he have to stay with us?" he heard Romeo, his half-brother, Mr. King's oldest son, challenge.

"You already know why," Mr. King shot back. "And I don't want to talk about it anymore. It's bad enough that I have to hear it from your mother all day."

"Well, if you weren't trying to be a playa…"

"What did you just say to me?"

A frustrated Mr. King, already on edge from this new arrangement and running late for work, was quickly losing patience with this unwelcomed lecture from his teenage son.

"Uh, nothing sir," Romeo squirmed under his father's warning glare.

"That's exactly what I thought! Now hurry up before you are late for school."

"Yes sir!" Romeo quickly grabbed up his book bag and escaped out the door.

David heard footsteps coming down the stairs into the basement; it was Mr. King.

"Let's go David; you don't want to be late for your first day of school. It's a miracle that I was even able to get you into this school, especially now that it's January and the second semester has already started. I hope you are a quick learner because this school's academics are pretty demanding, not like the public schools where you came from. Come on, let's go," Mr. King urged. "I'm late for a meeting. Everything is ready for you, just go to the main office and they will get you up to speed. Since I'm running late, Mrs. King is going to drive you; good luck."

David silently got dressed in record-breaking time. When he walked upstairs, there was a cold plate of food on the table.

"Guess I missed the memo about having family breakfast together," David mumbled to himself.

David put the plate of food in the microwave and was about to heat it up when he heard a series of violent honks from a car horn. Mrs. King was already in the car, and in no mood to wait. David grabbed a couple of pieces of cold toast off the table and ran out to the car. He snatched open the car door and started to apologize, "I'm sorry I didn't realize you were…"

Mrs. King threw up her hand, palm facing out toward David. Her lips were pressed tightly shut, and the brief look she allowed him quickly let him know she had nothing to say, and did not want to hear anything he had to say either. The unspoken tension between them filled the car like a thick cold, bitter fog.

Mrs. King stopped the car about a block away from the school and rattled off a few quick directions for David to fol-low, as he was going to have to walk the rest of the way. She offered a flimsy excuse that David had made her late for an appointment, but the truth was that she did not want to be seen dropping him off at school. She desperately wanted to avoid the potential of any interrogation at the school's PTA. However, David did not mind walking; he was relieved just to get out of that car. He quickly made his way to the school's campus and front office.

## Chapter 2
# First Day of School

For David, California was definitely unfamiliar. Everything seemed different, from the buildings to the food to the people — even the air seemed different. David was in a 'brand new world,' and he could feel it. It was his first day at his new school, Luas Prep, a private school owned by Luas Corp. It was a school for the wealthy and academically advanced, with a special program for students of the arts. The school was located on a prominent college campus, and advanced students had the opportunity to earn on-site college credits as well as sit in on some college level courses before they graduated.

Mr. King had a private practice as an accountant, and he had a share of clients on the Board of Directors of Luas Corp. Through these relationships, he was able to get all his boys into the school for nearly free, including David.

As David walked down the corridors, he felt the stares of the other students trained on him. It made him feel uneasy and completely out of place, like a prostitute in a convent. His usual casual attire did not blend well with the fashion show apparel the other kids were sporting: Fendi, DKNY, Armani, Burberry, Louis Vuitton, Gucci, Tommy Hilfiger... the alphabet of designer labels seemed endless. Out in the parking lot, the kids drove pricey late model sports cars and SUVs such as BMW, Porsche, and Lexus. It was a far cry from the public transportation he was used to. David was a long way from home and the way of life he left back in Brooklyn, NY.

When the class bell rang signaling lunch period, David headed to his locker to put away his books before hitting the cafeteria. He was only slightly unnerved when a couple of varsity athletes caught up to him and asked, "Hey man, you're new here right? What's your name?"

"David"

"Well David, just so you know, there's a toll charge here for use of our hallway. If you want to walk down it, you gotta pay up."

David shrugged, "Whatever," and tried to step around them.

"Whoa, where do think you're going?" One of the guys grabbed David from behind and threw him against the wall, pinning him while the other pounded David with bare-knuckle punches followed by a hard knee to David's stomach.

Further down the hall, David could see his half-brothers, Romeo and Trent, headed in his direction. For a moment, he felt a flash of relief, until he saw them smirk and turn the other way. Finally, the wanna be gang let him go with a final shove, throwing him onto the floor.

"Remember, tolls are due daily if you want to use this hallway!" they spat at David, while laughing and high-fiving each other before walking away.

David slowly pulled himself up, the pain from the beating making every move excruciating. He reached out to gather up the pile of scattered textbooks and paper. He involuntarily shrank back in instinctive fear when a shadow fell across the floor from behind him.

"Duuude, you just got beat DOWN! Does it hurt? 'Cause it looks like it really hurts. I mean your face looks…"

Slowly looking up, David saw with relief that the kid standing over him looked harmless. True Religion jeans, hi-top Fendis, Givenchy pullover, D&G watch, and sports cap cocked slightly to the side — totally California prep, perhaps, but harmless. JP was armed with a flip camcorder in his hand and was filming as if he was a freelance news reporter.

Grunting, David replied, "Yeah, so tell me something I don't know."

"Dude! Let me help you, man! I hate to see another brother down and out."

David, face slightly twisted in an expression of confusion, asked, "Wha… aren't you white?"

"Duuuude! What is color, man? Yo, yo, yo, my name is 'JP,' the hot MC from Cali," JP replied, throwing in a few Hip Hop moves for effect.

"Yeah, well my name is David, and I'm from the East Coast," David said slowly, with a hint of careful hesitation.

"Yo! I know all about the East Coast. What up son? Big, PD, Jay, Lauren…"

"JP! Can you please just point me to the bathroom so I can get cleaned up?" David interrupted.

"Oh, sure. My bad, dude, just follow me."

JP led David to the boy's bathroom, and took the liberty of scanning through David's personal belongings, including his class schedule, while David was busy washing his face and straightening his mussed clothes.

"Dang! Who are you Albert Einstein or something?" JP asked.

"What do you mean?"

"Man you are taking all kinds of excel… excel… smart kid courses!"

"Nah, no, it's not what you think. Those are just the courses they gave me."

Although he tried to play it off, the truth was that David loved learning, and he always leaned toward the most challenging courses a school had to offer, including extra-curricular programs. David's mother had always thought it was more important to spend money on activities that would stimulate her son's mind, and make him more marketable in his future, than popular video games or even designer labels. To her, the busier David was, the less prone he would be to seek out trouble in the streets while she was away at work.

Thus, she had placed him in every after-school program and class she could afford. David studied subjects ranging from music production, graphic design, computer programming and video editing to entrepreneur programs, marketing and even carpentry at the Reign Center, a division of Kingdom Reign Ministries, a non-profit organization committed to empowering teens and young adults to develop their purpose and strategy for a successful life. David had become a peer leader within that organization before he was forced to move to California.

"Well, what's up with weight lifting for gym class? You should take open gym like everyone else; it's an easy 'A'," JP offered.

"JP, you can't always take the easy way out. Besides, I've never done weight lifting before, and as you can see, I could use some muscle."

"Yeah, whatever. I think school is a waste of time. As for me, I am going to make it big in the music industry. Producin,' rappin,' I am going to have the hottest studio in the biz! You watch and see."

"Well, to me school is just a means to an end," David countered. "I am going to get as much out of it as I can on my way to making millions. The world needs successful people, so why not me?"

JP looked at David, "Hmm, I guess I never thought about it that way before. Hey Dave, if you need someone to show you around just yell at me."

David laughed, "I think you mean holla at me.  Yeah, man, I will.  Thanks.  How about a tour of the cafeteria for starters?"

Neither of them realized it that day, but David and JP were quickly about to become the best of friends.

# Chapter 3
# Michal

It had been three months since David left his old neighborhood and moved to his new home, three extremely frustrating months, with no signs or promise of improvement. He had made no new friends, besides JP of course, and to say things were uneasy at home was an understatement. His own brothers treated him as their own worst enemy, and Mr. and Mrs. King were tolerant, but obviously embarrassed by his existence, much less his presence in their home. School was the one place David seemed to have some control; he was good at school and was learning his way around campus fairly well — staying under the radar as to not standout. However, David spent much of his free time in the music rooms.

One particular afternoon, David had ducked out of the cafeteria early during lunch at school, and made his way to the music room. He sat down at the piano and lightly ran his fingers across the keys while fighting back tears. He missed his mom so much! His mother had always enjoyed listening to David play and sing. Slowly, he began a soft melody, a love song of praise to God. "I hope you can hear this," he whispered, "I love you, mom."

As he played, the melody soothed David's hurt like a healing salve. Tears streaming, David allowed himself to get lost in the music, playing that piano and joining it in song with the intensity of a musician performing for a sold out crowd at The Apollo. Unknown to David, his 'concert' was drawing quite a crowd just outside the door.

"Who is that?"

"Whoever it is, he's good!"

While the group of students continued murmuring and speculating the mystery, one girl slipped past them, and pressed inside the door. She stood there for a moment, taking in the sight of the young man enthusiastically pounding the piano keys, obviously oblivious to her, or anything else for that matter.

"Excuse me." She slowly approached him. "Hello? Um, excuse me," she called louder this time.

Startled by the sweet, but unexpected voice, David jumped and quickly swiped his tears.

"Sorry, I didn't hear you come in."

"Oh, that's okay. I just wanted to see who was up in here singing like Musiq Soulchild."

David laughed, "I don't know about all of that. Musiq is off the hook and I just..."

David looked up and locked eyes with the most beautiful woman he had ever seen. She was five-foot-four, with golden, silky brown skin, an exotic ethnic mix of black and Italian, her hair styled in a soft, short bob, hazel eyes framed with thick lashes — and her body was nothing short of incredible! She had an intriguing air about her too, no doubt classy, but mysterious and charismatic just the same. Wow!

David felt a rush much akin to a brain freeze, and he was speechless.

"Well, there is a group of people on the other side of that door that would beg to differ with you," she countered.

David looked toward the window in the door and saw a crowd of people staring in at them. The group of students outside began to cheer, some clapped and whistled while others offered a thumbs-up. David returned a shy smile. It was a pleasant surprise, but also kind of embarrassing.

"My name is Michalynn but everyone calls me Michal. And yours is?"

David, still preoccupied with the audience outside the door, almost did not hear her. "Huh? Oh, I'm sorry. My name is David."

David returned his attention to Michal, feeling awkward and trying not to stare, while carefully meeting her gaze. She was breathtaking, and he was officially lost in her beauty!

Finally, after a short, uncomfortable silence, Michal said, "So, uh, I'd better be getting to class. I just wanted to say that I enjoyed your song."

Michal turned to leave, then stopped short turning back to David. "By the way, if that's an original, you may want to copy-right it before some fine sista' decides to record it. Talk to you later," she winked.

"Whoa, wait! You sing?"

"Bye, David. It was nice meeting you." Michal smiled and strolled out of the room in pure diva fashion.

"Michal, you ain't right girl!" David smiled to himself. "Dang, I've gotta get my act together!"

He could still smell the faint fragrance of her enticing perfume even after she left the room. The girl not only made his day, she had just made his month! David decided that perhaps it was time he worked toward making the best of his new situation, starting with a cleanup of his attitude, and most certainly his appearance.

Since his mom's funeral, David had let himself go; he had no drive to care about how he looked anymore. He had never worn many of the name brand clothes or

designer shoes, but he had always managed to look good. Catching his reflection
in a store window as he walked home
that afternoon, he was a bit taken aback
by the guy that was staring back at him.

Tugging at his disheveled shirt, and
frowning in disgust, David said to himself,
"I have GOT to get rid of this afro." The
problem was that David was stuck in sub-
urbia and had no idea of how to find someone that could cut and twist hair. When he
got home, he found one of the twins playing a video game in the den. Against his
better judgment he asked him, "Hey, Trent,
where is the nearest barbershop?"

Trent, never looking up from his
game, shot back a quick reply. "Uh, sure,
no problem, man, I'll hook you up."

"Okay, thanks."

Trent said, "Man don't even worry
about it, that's what brothers are for."

David smiled and made his way downstairs to his meager quarters to start on his
homework and hopefully get a good
night's sleep. He was looking forward to
finding out more about Michal and talking
with her some more.

## Chapter 4
# Brotherly Love

Later that night, David was startled awake by three pairs of hands forcefully snatching him from his bed. Out of the corner of his eye, he could see the green light of the clock beaming 2:04 a.m. He could not see their faces clearly in the dark, but he instantly recognized their hushed voices. It was his brothers, Romeo and the twins, Derrick and Trent. Quickly, they pinned David down and bound his hands and feet with duct tape, then placed a strip across his mouth so that no one could hear his cries for help.

"So, you wanted a haircut, huh? Well, welcome to our barbershop, you little punk! I don't know why your little ho for

a mutha, no family havin, no class..."
Romeo mocked David.

By now, Trent had already shaved a patch out of David's hair down to the scalp. David fiercely struggled against the duct tape that bound his wrists. The brothers did not realize that the tape had a bit of slack, and were caught by surprise when David broke his hands free.

"Ouch!" cried Trent as David threw a hard punch against his jaw. David spun around and kicked Derrick in the stomach, knocking the wind out of him and causing him to stumble backwards. Romeo leapt at David from behind, throwing him down on the bed. David took advantage of Romeo's stunned distraction as the bed frame gave way with a loud crack. Quickly, he grabbed Romeo and flipped him over, catching him in an unforgiving chokehold.

David shouted, "If you ever disrespect my mother again, I promise to God I'll..."

Mr. and Mrs. King came running down the stairs. "What is going on down here?!" they shouted in unison.

Mrs. King quickly pounced on David, pulling him off Romeo. Giving him a rough shove, she turned to face him, anger flashing like daggers in her eyes. "What is wrong with you?" she screamed. "We take you in, give you a better life than that ghetto you came from, and this is how you repay us, acting like some kind of gangster for hire? Let me tell you, this is not the projects, you little hoodlum, and my boys have done nothing to war-rant this sort of attack in the middle of the night!" To her husband, "Jesse, I want him out of this house! You need to put a leash on that little bastard. My mother always said if you lay down with dogs, you'll get up with fleas. Who knew I would have a flea in my house."

David broke in, "Mr. King, I can leave. It ain't nothing to me! I don't want to be where I'm not wanted."

"Leave then!" yelled Romeo.

"Shut up, Romeo!" shouted Mr. King. "Nobody is going anywhere. Boys, go to your rooms, NOW! I will deal with you tomorrow."

The boys quickly made their way up the stairs without another word. They had never seen their father this angry before.

"Jesse I WANT HIM OUT!!!" Mrs. King screamed.

Mr. King turned on his wife, almost seeming to forget that David was still in the room. "No, Linda! You are always defending those boys, even when they are wrong, but not this time. You are not going to take your anger towards me out on David. And I'm sick and tired of your self-righteous attitude when the truth is you are not all that innocent either, honey. Just because I never said anything about the paperwork I found from the clinic after your all girls vacation to Jamaica that second year we were married, doesn't mean that I don't know about it. At least I take care of my responsibilities and don't just make them go away.... Why are you looking so surprised? Go to bed, and I will be up momentarily."

Mrs. King, flushed with embarrassment and struggling to find words to explain, muttered, "But, honey…"

"Don't honey me, just go." Mr. King said with disgust.

After she left, Mr. King looked at David and sighed ruefully, "David I want to apologize for what happened tonight. What I need for you to understand is that this is not easy for any of us, and I know it's especially not easy for you. Up until a few months ago, the only people in our family who knew about my being unfaithful to Mrs. King were Mrs. King and me. So to have another child enter the picture just opened up a whole new can of worms, not to mention emotions that have been suppressed for years. However, this is a strong family. I know you couldn't tell it by tonight's actions, but we will survive and be the better for it. I don't know if you and I will have a traditional father/son bond, but I do want us to at least try and be friends. And, as a friend, I would suggest that you shave the rest of your hair off and start over, because you can't pull the girls with a hole in your fro, bro!" With that, Mr. King laughed and laughed, as if he had just told the funniest joke ever.

David just shook his head and grabbed a couple of 2x4 planks to prop up his broken bed frame. However, David could not sleep; he had a sudden burst of energy after Mr. King left to head back upstairs. So, he decided to clean up the entire basement. By the time he finished, it looked like it was ready for a much needed home makeover. The place was swept spotless, tools were in their respectful places, and with everything cleaned up, the downstairs looked massive. David finally managed to get about an hour's worth of sleep, but when he woke up, he knew it was going to be an energy drink kind of a day.

———◆◆———

The next morning, David almost wished he had heeded Mr. King's advice from the night before to shave his head when he was greeted with smirks and muffled giggles at the breakfast table. David was wearing a backwards baseball cap, along with a hooded sweatshirt, to hide the bald spot. He wondered which would draw more attention, the bald spot or the sweatshirt.

Later, at school, David decided, "The hoodie, yep, the hoodie," when he heard JP hollering at him at the top of his lungs. "What in the world happened to you?"

David shushed JP, "Keep your voice down. I don't want to talk about it."

"But dude, you look like a serial killer. A *hot* serial killer. Don't you know this is Cali? It's warm outside dude. At least take the hood down, or the sweatshirt off." JP grabbed the hood of David's sweatshirt and yanked it down, revealing the prominent bald spot. "Oh, NO! Who in the world carved you up like that, man? Dude you look like a chia pet gone wrong, I mean…"

"JP," David warned, "leave it alone! I DO NOT WANT TO TALK ABOUT IT!"

"Geez, Dave, okay. That's all you had to say. Man, what's wrong with you?"

"My family is what's wrong with me. I just wanna, ugh!"

"Dave, don't even sweat it. Things have a way of coming full circle. Trust me, just be cool and you'll see. But I need you to come with me, like right now."

"What? Why?"

"Dude, just follow me right now."

David followed behind JP first through one door, then another and another, down into what seemed like a tunnel. David wanted to turn and go back, but he was not sure he knew his way out, so, reluctantly, he stuck with following JP.

Finally, they reached a large metal door. JP knocked three times and the door flew open. They stepped through the door into a large room, greeted by a group of loud, boisterous male voices, "JP!" David quickly counted seven men. It appeared that they were all just hanging out, with four of them huddled around a table playing cards.

JP addressed the group, "Guys, this is my boy Dave."

The men welcomed David like a long lost friend.

David leaned toward JP and whispered, "JP, who are these guys and what are we doing here?"

JP draped an arm across David's shoulders and replied, "Well, these guys are the backbone of this fine establishment of higher learning. They take care of the buildings, grounds, and security of this place. This is their haven, so feel welcome. But there is a toll charge — they love junk food and movies." With that, JP reached inside his bag, pulled out a pair of bootleg DVD movies, and handed them to the men playing cards.

"Now Dave, have a seat, we don't have much time," JP said, pointing David to an empty chair. "I can't have my boy going around school embarrassing us with that Frankenstein do, it just ain't right."

Before David could react, JP had whipped out a pair of barbershop clippers seemingly from thin air. "JP, no man I'm good," David started backing way. "You are not going to touch my head with those clippers; it's not going to happen."

"Dude, just trust me."

"No, JP!"

JP sighed, "Dave, normally I wouldn't do this, but we are pressed for time. So... fellas, hold him down!"

"JP, NOOOOOOOOOOOOOOOOO!!!!"

## Chapter 5
# Payback

David was very self-conscious about his new haircut. He went to his first period class, but found it hard to concentrate; it seemed his mind was in a thousand different places. He flirted with thoughts of running away, but where would he go? Then he thought about what his mom always told him, "Life will try to beat you down, and it will if you let it; but you have the power to beat life and make it serve you. You are the king of your world, and if you don't like what you see, change it! Don't complain, change! But always remember that the change begins with you. You can't change people, but you can change you, and eventually those around you will change. Choose — the choice is yours."

David smiled to himself, "I guess mom knew days like this were coming."

At lunch, David waited for JP at a table outside. JP had told David that he had a surprise for him. David could use some cheering up. He was still fuming about his brothers and Mrs. King. As for Mr. King, he had not decided how he felt about him just yet. For so long, David had wished he knew who his dad was, and yet he was angry because his dad was never there. However, if he was honest, he was optimistic about the possibilities of having a real dad and not just another 'father figure.'

David's thoughts were interrupted when a soft hand playfully caressed the back of his head.

"Oh, excuse me, I'm sorry. I thought you were someone else. I was looking for this guy that sings like Musiq Soulchild and has a wild head of hair. You bear a remarkable resemblance, but I must say that you are much finer than he is." With that, Michal leaned close and seductively whispered against David's ear, "The low-cut mohawk is definitely working for you, mmmm hmmm." She stood and wiggled her fingers, "Bye, David."

David sat dumbfounded, spellbound as he watched her slip away. Several minutes later, he was still staring in the direction she disappeared when, SMACK!

David's hand instinctively flew to the back of his head to massage the sting from the unsuspected blow.

"What's up, Woodstock?"

It was the same two guys from the other day back for more, this time with a couple of friends. They were the school's 'star' athletes David had learned, varsity Lacrosse players. Luas Corp Prep was known for its championship Lacrosse team. David grimaced and put his right hand in his pocket, bracing himself for the pending attack.

Just as they sat down and leaned toward David, he heard a familiar voice call, "Dude! You need to leave my boy alone!"

It was JP!

"Uh, oh," David thought to himself, "we are both about to get beat down."

The guys calmly stood, glared at David, then started to walk away without saying another word.

David, with a new confidence, jumped to his feet and called out, "Hey!" The players all turned back. The ringleader of the group began to edge closer to David, his eyes flashing with a mocking dare. David swung with all of his might and landed a hard fist to the guy's jaw. The ringleader fell to the ground; he was out cold!

"Don't you ever put your hands on me again!" David warned, and then proceeded to drop a roll of quarters that he had concealed with his fist onto the guy's chest. The others just paused, looked up at JP, and walked away. The school grounds were dead silent for a moment, and then all of a sudden everyone in the vicinity began to cheer like a war had just been won.

JP hollered, "Dude!" and pulled out his flip camera and started filming. He held up his hand to silence the crowd, and then turned to David and said, "Now that you have successfully knocked out this bully and ended his tyrannical reign, what will you do next?"

David responded, "Go to Disney World?"

The crowd erupted again with cheers and laughter, David and JP gave each other high fives and quickly made their way to the other side of campus before the campus security showed up.

"What just happened, why didn't they fight back?" David wondered. "Man, what was that all about?" he asked JP.

"Whatever do you mean my young Jedi?" JP responded sarcastically.

"Why did those guys stop dead in their tracks when you showed up?"

"Oh, you've just gotta put some bass in your voice and people will respond. You should try it sometime."

"JP?" David arched his eyes at JP, not convinced.

"I'm telling you, it's all in how you talk to people. That, and maybe I might have some dirt on them that they don't want anyone to know about."

"Really?"

"I said I *might*. You know the threat of being found out is always worse than actually being found out. That's why I don't have any secrets, that way no one can use them against me. Make sense?"

"Yeah, amazingly that makes a lot of sense. So what's this surprise?"

"Well, the first one is, don't eat the school food, it will kill you. So I got you the best chicken sandwich on the planet." JP whipped out a white paper sack with red lettering, "Chick-fil-A baby! That's your favorite right?"

"Yeah man," David laughed, "one of them."

"And the second surprise, well, I can't tell you right now, but call me tonight and we'll talk about it."

"Okay then," David agreed, eyes full of question, but quickly forgotten as he bit into the juicy, spicy chicken sandwich. Ah yeah, it was high on his list of favorite foods.

Later that afternoon, when David got home from school, he found Mr. and Mrs. King waiting for him. Mrs. King was visibly upset.

Mr. King firmly questioned him, "David, what happened at school today?"

"I'm sorry?" replied David. "I don't know what you are referring to." David was afraid that they must have found out about the fight outside of the cafeteria where he knocked out the school's star Lacrosse player, however he was not about to admit to anything until the evidence brought against him left him no choice.

Mrs. King uncrossed her arms, looking as if she were ready to pounce on David. "You know what you did, you little hoodlum!" she yelled.

David managed to keep his cool, although inside his emotions were running wild with fear and confusion. He directed his attention to his father, "Mr. King, I honestly don't know what you all are talking about."

"David where were you between 8:30 and 10:45 this morning?"

David breathed a sigh of relief; the fight was much later than that. "Oh, I had first period class from 8:30 to 9:15, and then I was in the office with my guidance counselor taking some placement tests. I may be able to graduate early," he added.

Mr. King's stern expression relaxed, "Wow, that's awesome David! That's great news, I am so proud... ooofff."

Mrs. King had elbowed Mr. King in the side, shooting him a look that told him they were not there to celebrate.

Mr. King cleared his throat, "David have you seen your brothers today?"

"No, sir," David answered slowly, confused as to where this was leading. "I hardly ever see them at school, and like I said, I was in the guidance office taking tests all day, except for first period and lunch."

Mrs. King shouted, "You're a liar! You know what you did, and so help me God, I will..."

"Linda, let me handle this," Mr. King broke in.

"Well handle it! Handle it, Jesse! Are you going to handle it like you handled that whore?"

David stiffened, "Mr. King I am doing my best to be respectful to your wife, but nobody is going to talk about my mother like that! Especially not a woman that can't keep her husband satisfied at home." He narrowed his eyes at Mrs. King, "You know what they say, the darker the berry, the sweeter the juice. Mr. King, it must be tough to be stuck with an old bag of lemons at home."

Mrs. King flushed with fury, "And you are just going to sit there and let him talk to me like that?!" she spat, looking back and forth between David and a stunned Mr. King before storming out. "Well, I never!"

"Maybe if you did, you wouldn't be in this predicament!" David called behind her.

He could hear the King's bedroom door slam shut as he stormed off to the basement, slamming his door too.

Mr. King sat stiffly on the edge of the sofa, now alone in the living room. He dropped his head in his hands and mournfully sighed. "What have I done?" he asked the empty room. "I never thought the choices I made in my youth would come back to haunt me like this. What now?"

He reached inside his pocket, pulled out his cell phone, and started dialing.

Later that night at dinner, the King boys came to the table wearing hooded sweatshirts and sunglasses.

"You know we don't wear hats, hoodies, or sunglasses at the table, boys. Take them off," Mr. King said.

Slowly, the King boys removed their hoods and sunglasses, only to reveal that they were completely hairless! David almost choked on his food as he fought hard not to laugh. They looked like they were trying out for the leading role in the 1995 blockbuster movie, 'Powder,' with no hair at all, as in slick baldheads with no eyebrows, no eyelashes, nothing. Their heads and the areas around their eyes were speckled with little red bumps, like a rash.

"What happened to you guys?" David asked in disbelief.

"Oh you know what happened, why you…" Romeo stopped short in mid-sentence as his father, clearing his throat to catch his son's attention, shot him a stern warning look.

Mr. King put his fork down and met eyes with everyone at the table, "This ends tonight!" he demanded. "First of all, I called the school and David is telling the truth, he was with the guidance counselor all morning and most of the afternoon." Mr. King turned his attention to David, "Great job by the way, David. The counselor told me how advanced you are in your studies. Keep up the good work. Secondly, he looked back at the rest of his family, "we are all family here, like it or not, and we are going to ACT like it! I don't care if you have to pretend, we are going to be civil and treat each other with respect. Do you hear me, and do you understand?"

"Yes, sir," they all mumbled in unison.

"Now, David," he continued, "if I do find out that you had anything to do with this, or if you pull any pranks against my boys in the future, I will send you off to military school so fast it will make your head spin, and you will stay there until you graduate. As for the rest of you, the downstairs is David's domain — his personal space for him to do whatever he wants with it, and it's off limits to everyone in this house unless you have express permission from David or myself."

All three of the King boys and Mrs. King smirked smugly at the threat. David simply got up from the table, put his dishes in the sink, and retired to his room. He knew that anger would not fix this situation, but he needed a plan in order to be successful. He felt like Mr. King had just given the rest of the family permission and incentive to set him up for failure and have him shipped off to military school.

Minutes later, David heard a knock at his door, the outdoor entrance to his room downstairs. Without waiting for a response, JP came barging into the room, overcome with laughter.

"Dude, why didn't you call me?" he asked.

David was clueless, "Call you about what?"

"My surprise!"

Then it hit him. "You? What, you mean that was you? Oh man, JP. My family is blaming me and threatening to ship me off to military school. Seriously, I have enough to deal with here without you adding to it. As much as I hate being here, this is all I've got right now; I can't afford to screw it up."

JP sobered, "Dave, my bad man. I'm sorry, I just wanted you to know I've got your back. I didn't mean to get you in trouble." JP paused, looking a little uneasy and confused, "You know, you sure are one different type of dude, man. Most folks would've been all over the revenge."

"JP, don't get me wrong, it was funny," David grinned. "But people like that are not even worth the effort. Besides, they'll eventually create their own demise, trust me on that. It's just that, well, right now, I really have to be extra careful, you know?"

"Sure Dave, just as long as you know I've got you."

"Thanks, JP."

JP nodded, gazing in silence at the floor. A moment later, David gave a small laugh, "I've got to give you credit, JP, you are one crazy dude. Wait! Did I just say dude?"

## Chapter 6
# Luas Corp

It was April, and things were starting to warm up. David knew it was time for some fresh kicks and a wardrobe upgrade. With life at home being shaky at best, David decided that he needed to be as independent as possible, and for that, a job was key. He was used to fending for himself, and he hated being at home, so David applied for a position working at Luas Corp's headquarters cleaning the offices at night. David was responsible for cleaning the first floor offices, as well as the bathrooms on the executive wing. Luas Corp was a major corporation and the largest employer in Orange County. They had their hands in everything from television, film and entertainment, to global real estate.

Luas Corp also owned the largest building in Orange County. Not only was it the largest building, but it was also considered a work of art, having been featured in a number of magazines as well as TV shows.

David had been employed at Luas Corp for about a month when he went to work one Friday evening and noticed interior decorating trucks parked in front of the building. After he had finished the first floor and was making his way to the executive wing, he met one of the workers coming off the elevator.

David greeted him, "Hey, what's going on?"

"Apparently someone wasn't pleased with the look of their million dollar office, so we are changing it," the man replied, his voice dripping with sarcastic disdain.

"Are you serious?!"

"Yup."

"But this set up is absolutely beautiful."

"I know, but when you have money to burn you can do whatever you want."

"I guess. Hey, let me ask you a question, what are they going to do with the old stuff?"

"Throw it away, my friend."

"Get outta here! Are you serious?"

"Yep, we are taking it to the dump tonight."

"But it's practically brand new."

"I know."

David paused as he contemplated his next words. "Let me ask you another question."

"Go ahead," the man nodded.

"What are the chances of me taking it?"

"Sorry, pal. We're not allowed to do that; I could get fired."

"Come on man," David urged, "you have to pass by my house on your way out of town in order to get to the dump."

A little more encouragement and four hundred dollars later, David was the proud owner of some fine office furniture and décor.

It was the beginning of the weekend and the King family was away visiting Mrs. King's parents, (David was not invited of course), and they would not be back until Sunday. David knew he would need help getting it all downstairs and set-up before his family got home, so he sent JP a text asking him to meet him at the house after he got off. After work, David rushed home, where he found JP already there waiting for him.

"Dude, what's going on? I thought it was some kind of emergency or something."

"No man, I have some furniture being delivered and I need your help to get it moved in without alerting anyone."

"Dude, it's like one in the morning, man. You know this is my poker night and my hand was *hot*. You are so lucky I like you — you owe me big!"

"I know, I know, but wait until you see this set up, man."

"Aiight den, son!" JP whooped.

"Shhh! Not so loud, and you really need to stick with 'dude.' Yo, here he comes. Oh, by the way, what's with the bandage around your wrist?"

"Awww, man, I burned myself trying to iron today, it's nothing. Come on, let's get this stuff off the truck."

"Cool," agreed David.

The truck backed into the drive, and David and JP leapt on the back, unloading the carpet, desk, chairs, lamps, and other furniture and décor. David had designated space in the backyard for them to place the furniture until he could get it inside and arranged like he wanted. Once it was unloaded, they covered everything up with a tarp.

David was so excited and eager that he asked the deliveryman, "Do you think it would be possible to lay this carpet tonight?"

"Are you kidding me?" the man scoffed.

"I'll throw in an extra hundred bucks."

"Buddy, I don't care if you throw in an extra five hundred dollars, the answer is 'NO!'"

Tired and grumpy after a long day, the man was ready to get home and get some sleep. He had no desire to stay on and help a couple teenagers lay carpet the rest of the night.

JP jumped in, "Dave, don't worry about it. I have a cousin that lays carpet with his dad; I'm sure I can get him to do it."

The man said, "See, there you go. Your boy has a cousin that lays carpet."

"Thanks man, I really appreciate it. Here's an extra hundred anyway for all the trouble."

"You didn't have to do that," the man replied as he hesitantly accepted the money.

"I know, but you went out on a limb for me."

The man opened the door to climb back in his truck, then stopped and turned back to David. "Listen kid, there's a 42-inch plasma TV in the truck that's chipped. The screen is fine, but for the kind of clients we have, we can't sell it. If you want it, it's yours. There's also a hundred-gallon saltwater fish tank in there as well; it has everything you need except for the fish.  But if anyone asks you, I was never here and we have never met, got it?"

"Yeah, of course, sure.  But why are you doing this?"

"Kid, there's just something about you.  I don't know what it is, but stay true to yourself, don't let anyone stop you from being great, and don't let your greatness stop you from being you.  Now get this stuff off the truck, and be quick about it.  I've got to go."

———◆———

That weekend, David and JP worked all hours day and night to get the carpet laid and set the furniture up.  JP had called in some favors and had a makeshift construction/moving crew to help with all the work.  It felt like an episode on 'DIY Network.'  The carpet was so plush, it felt like you were walking on clouds.  The office desk was an L-shaped dark mahogany, like something you would see on Donald Trump's show 'The Apprentice.'

In addition, there was a mahogany board-room table that could seat ten, track lighting with dimmers, and two deep leather chairs to round it out.

Naturally, David was also excited about his brand new HDTV. By the time they finished, they were completely exhausted, but the space looked amazing! It was like a New York City penthouse apartment. David thought, "I just need to get a nice bedroom set and couch, and the downstairs would be complete."

Sitting on the front porch lost in his daydreams, David did not notice JP skipping down the steps to the driveway. Suddenly, loud beeping noises from a big truck backing up broke David away from his thoughts. He looked up to see JP directing a flatbed truck backwards down the driveway. On it was an entire bedroom set from Ikea. David was in shock. JP just looked over at him and grinned and said, "I know people."

Later, after the new bedroom set was unloaded and arranged, David and JP sat in the plush leather chairs, taking in David's new set up. "Dude, this is tight," whistled JP admiringly.

David said, "JP, I can't thank you enough, man. This is too much. Anytime you need a place to hang, man, consider this your home."

"Yeah, I may have to take you up on that, dude. Me and my dad, we don't get along so good. He ignores me, and I try to stay out of his way. It seems to work best like that; otherwise we're at each other's throats."

JP laid his head back and stared at the ceiling as he continued, "My old man never wanted me, dude. Story goes that he was on his way to West Point when my mom discovered she was pregnant with me. He tried to get her to get an abortion, but she refused. He went on to West Point, tried to attend college full time while supporting her, but soon discovered he couldn't manage to do both, so he dropped out. Came back and married her. He basically gave up on his life's dream, and he blames me for it. He started drinking heavily about seven years ago. When he gets drunk, he likes to get violent, beating on me and my mom."

"Oh, man, how come no one says anything?" asked David.

"Dude, out here it's all about appearances, and who would believe us anyway? My dad heads up the ROTC program and is a deacon at our church. If anyone knew what was really going on, he would lose his job and his position at the church, making it worse for us at home. One good thing has come out of it though."

"Oh yeah, what's that?"

"It's given me a whole lot to rap about."

David laughed, "Yeah I feel you on that. Music is my outlet as well. I wish I had a place to lay some tracks."

"Yeah, studio time out here is crazy expensive. I used to have a hook up at the studio at school."

"You used to?" David questioned.

"Yeah, I was dating the girl that was in charge of scheduling, and she used to hook me up with free time. I just had to bring my own cd's to burn and handle my own engineering. Technically, everything done in the studio has to be 'school related.'"

"So what happened?"

"Well, let's just say there is no way to reconcile."

"Come on, man, just tell me."

"It's complicated."

"Aw, man, come on! Tell me what happened."

"Okay, okay, but yo, this has to stay between us. When I started dating this girl, I was kinda messin' around with someone else on the side." JP sighed, "I can't believe I am telling you this. So when I started dating Sharon, I told the other woman that we had to stop screwing around, it was all about the sex, the passion, getting my freak on, smackin that…"

"JP! Come back!"

"Sorry dawg, had a flash back. So anyway, I really liked Sharon and things were going well, but she would never let me come over and meet the parents. They were apparently going through a rough time and the mom was suspected of having an affair. You know, family drama stuff."

"Was she?"

"Hold on, man, I'm getting to that. So, one evening we had parent/teacher conferences at the school. Sharon and I were in the studio, I was letting her listen to my tracks. On our way out of the studio, we could see the parents and the teachers talking in the classrooms. When I walked past one of the classrooms, I spotted the other woman that I had been messing around with."

"Hold up, what do you mean you saw her in the classroom?"

"Dude, she's a little bit older."

"A little?"

JP ignored the question and continued his story, "I tried to rush and get off campus, but Sharon had to use the bathroom. As I was waiting for her, I heard this woman calling my name… Jean Paul."

"Wait, wait," David broke in, "Jean Paul?"

"Yes, Jean Paul, and if you tell anyone I WILL KILL YOU. Like I was saying, while I was waiting, this woman came walking toward me with this low cut, short skirt, business suit on. She pressed her body up against mine. I was speechless, man, as she cornered me in the hallway and began to whisper things in my ear that you are too young to hear. Then she actually slid her tongue in my ear and whispered 'Don't you miss my...' and, dude, at that very moment Sharon walked out of the bathroom with this look of complete disbelief and says, 'MOM?!' Oh, she smacked the hell out of me, and all I could say was, 'I didn't know, I didn't know!'"

"Why didn't you try and deny it?"

"Dude, even if I could have denied it, with the state Mr. Good Stuff was in, I would have been arrested for perjury. That was the last time I ever spoke to Sharon or her mom."

"Daaang! Yo, I'm usually the king of smoothing things over, but this one might be out of my league. Do you still like her?"

"Yeah man, she was the first girl that had the entire package. She really understood me and I understood her. But how do you get over your boyfriend doing your mom?"

"For real! I dunno, maybe we can figure something out."

"Figure something out with the studio or with Sharon?"

"Both."

"Well, if we could figure something out with the studio, we could make a whole lot of C – A – S – H! Luas Corp is killing artists with studio fees. Actually, Sharon could help us if she wasn't so pissed at me for sleeping with her mom. Maaan! That woman is so supple and tender, the way she could work her…"

"JP!"

"Oh, sorry. Had another flash back."

"Uh, so the first thing you have to do is stop having flash backs about Sharon's mom if you ever want to get Sharon back."

JP sat thoughtfully for a moment, "You know, I think you might be right."

"So JP, how long are you going to make me wait to hear these tracks of yours?"

"Man, I got my iPod right here. It's just a matter of if your speakers can handle the hotness that's about to come through them."

"Hook it up man," David urged, nodding in the direction of his 'new' stereo equipment.

JP connected his iPod to David's stereo system and they listened to track after track after track. David tried not to let his emotions show, but the music drew him in. He closed his eyes and let his head bob with the rhythm. JP's production was off the charts, and his flow was nice. David and JP free-styled over the tracks for hours. They knew that even though they didn't have any real equipment, money or connections, they were about to embark on a partnership that was going to change the entertainment industry forever. They sketched a plan out on paper, and were about to put a time line together, when JP looked at the clock.

"Duuude, do you know what time it is?"

"Nine o'clock, Sunday morning," David replied matter-of-factly.

"Yo, I gotta go!"

"Where are you going?"

"I have to be at church."

"Oh, yeah. What church?"

"OCCC — Orange County Community Church. Mr. and Mrs. King go there, everyone goes there it seems. The pastor is pretty cool, but the music sucks."

"Are you serious? They are usually gone when I wake up on Sundays. I thought they were just running errands or something."

"Yeah dude, I was wondering why I hadn't seen you there."

"So, what were you saying about the music?" David quickly changed the subject.

"We have all the instruments we need, but this old lady that plays the organ, I swear, man, she's like a hundred-and-ten-years-old. You should come see it for yourself."

## Chapter 7
# O.C.C.C.

When David walked into the church, it was almost like attending a funeral. All the teenagers hovered in the back pews talking and laughing, and some were even dozing.

JP sat at the drums, trying to liven up the service. The organist looked as if she had just sucked on a whole pound of lemons, and was visibly annoyed, muttering under her breath. She played every song at least two speeds slower than called for. It all just seemed so… so morbid, nothing like the churches from David's old hometown, which were lively, upbeat, and the music was off the hook!

David took a pew beside one of the dozing youth in the back; he fully understood and empathized with his slumbering pew neighbor, until the pastor took the pulpit. The pastor announced the subject of the Sunday morning service, 'destiny.'

"Hmm," thought David, "this could be interesting."

The pastor began, "The road to destiny can be a rough road, full of twists and turns, ups and downs, and sometimes you just can't see where it is taking you, but if you stay on it, it will ultimately bring you to your destination. Some people may not be able to complete the journey with you, but you must finish your course. For in finishing your course you will empower others to finish theirs."

David sat up straight, taking it all in. It felt as if the preacher was talking right to him. As he continued, David was taken back to the final moments he shared with his mom before she passed. "Son, I may not be with you physically," she had told him, "but I will always be in your thoughts and in your heart, and when times get rough, look to God for your help and strength. God's hand is on you son. Keep God first, and He will never leave you or forsake you, even when you make mistakes. That's when His love shines through the brightest, to guide you during your darkest moments."

The pastor continued, "Some of you have been going through a rough time, feeling a lot of pressure. You don't know which way is up. Perhaps you feel like giving up and throwing in the towel, but I've got good news! The best is yet to come. If you need strength from the Lord, come forward right now and let us pray for you."

The next thing David knew, he was walking down the aisle.

"That's right son, come on."

David could feel the eyes of everyone in the church burrowing into him. Mr. King sat staring in disbelief, as Mrs. King buried her face in her hands and mumbled under her breath.

The pastor reached toward David, "Welcome, son. My name is Pastor Nate, and you are?"

"David."

"Glad to have you, David. Do you know Jesus as your Savior?"

"No sir, I don't."

"Would you like to fix that? Do you want to give your heart to Jesus?"

"Yes sir. I think I do."

"Well David, Romans 10:9-10 says that if you confess with your mouth, 'Jesus is Lord,' and believe in your heart that God raised him from the dead, you will be saved. I promise you, David, your life will never be the same again."

Pastor Nate began to pray with David, and as they prayed, David could feel the burdens of heavy pains lifting. The pain from not being loved by his new family, the pain of his mom dying, the pain of not being accepted. He cried as the darkness inside him found release.

Pastor Nate patted David's back reassuringly, and after allowing him time to regain his composure, asked him loud enough for the rest of the congregation to hear "So David, where are you from?"

The entire King family watched in horror, terrified of what David's response would reveal.

David turned slightly to face the congregation, "I am from Brooklyn, New York. My mom passed away about four months ago. I had no where to go, and the Kings heard about my situation, and being the wonderful family that they are, they took me in and showed me what a true family life could be like."

A roar of praise erupted from the crowd as Pastor Nate turned towards the Kings and motioned for them to stand.

"See, saints of God, this is what I have been preaching and teaching about, showing the true love of God in a practical way. Going beyond our comfort zones and showing the world what true love is through unselfish kindness! King family, please come forward."

As the King family walked to the front of the church, the entire congregation leapt to their feet and offered them a standing ovation.

Mrs. King was all smiles as she snatched the microphone and began to perform, "Praise the Lord, saints! Truly, it's a privilege to be a vessel of honor in the hands of God. I am just so thankful that we have had the opportunity to be a blessing in David's life. It is so rewarding to share the gifts and blessings that have been bestowed upon us and share it with someone else. I just get so choked up when I think that God could actually use someone like me." She pressed her hand against her chest and sniffed.

Mr. King was embarrassed by his wife's performance, but he managed to maintain a steady façade. At the end of the service, the King's were swarmed by the church members offering their congratulations and admiration. Mrs. King just basked in the attention and praise.

## Chapter 8
# Conflicted

After church, David and JP were walking home when JP asked David about what happened when Pastor Nate prayed for him.

"JP, I don't really know, but I feel good. I mean all the anger I had for my half brothers and Mr. and Mrs. King left, especially towards Mrs. King. I don't know what Pastor Nate did to me, but whatever it was it worked."

"Maybe I should get some of that. Yeah dude, your stepmom is a piece of work. It was a shame how she performed in church today."

David laughed, "Tell me about it, but you know what, it didn't even bother me.

She has to deal with God herself. JP, I just feel free, man."

"Dave, I wish I could have that same feeling towards my dad. There are times when I just want to..." JP kicked the dirt as hard as he could.

"JP, it's okay, I understand. You know, you should talk to Pastor Nate. Holding all that anger inside is not good; nobody should have that kind of control over you."

"Yeah, I guess you're right. I gotta let this thing go. But, dude, when you see this so called man beating on your mom and she can't do anything about it, ugh!" JP shot at the air with his thumb and index finger, "It makes you want to blast the punk."

"I feel you... but you aren't thinking about actually doing it, are you?" David hesitated, and then asked again, "Are you?"

"Dave, do you really want to know?" JP stopped short and looked hard at David, "Let me show you something."

JP opened the backpack he carried around with him, and pulled out a black

Glock 9mm handgun with hollow point bullets.

"JP, what are you thinking?" David asked in alarm.

"Dave, it's either going to be me or him. I can't continue living like this; one of us has to go — one way or another."

"JP, suicide is never an option, and neither is murder; nobody is worth you throwing your life away for."

"I know, Dave, but..." JP's cell began to vibrate. Staring at the screen in disbelief, he told David, "I can't believe it, man, it's a text from Sharon's mom!"

"What's it say?"

JP looked up at David, "It says, 'Call me — 911!'"

"Yo, how long has it been since you last talked to her?"

"About a year."

"What do you think it's about?"

"I dunno, but I'm about to find out."

JP hit the call back button, and held the phone against his ear.

"Hello... Jean Paul?" a panicked voice answered on the other end.

"Yeah, it's me. Hello? I can barely hear you."

"Can you hear me now? Jean Paul, Sharon was in a terrible car accident, and now she's..."

"Wait, you're breaking up! What about Sharon? She's what? Dead?"

JP dropped the phone, his face frozen with a look of shock and horror.

David shook JP's arm, "What happened? What's wrong?"

"Sharon is dead," JP uttered, barely above a whisper.

"What? Are you sure?"

"Her mom just said that she was in an accident, and then she said Sharon is dead!"

JP slammed his backpack on the ground, swung about and screamed, "NOOOOOOO!" then took off running.

David called after JP, "Hold up man, wait!" However, JP kept going, never looking back. David picked up JP's phone and backpack. He thought this would give him a good opportunity to check out JP's gun. David also decided he was going to make sure JP had the story straight. He kept walking until he was sure he had a good signal, and then he hit redial on the phone.

"Hello, Jean Paul?"

"No, this is David a friend of JP's. I am so sorry to hear about the passing of your daughter."

Sharon's mom screamed, "What! OH GOD! Not my baby! Please God, no! I just left her, the doctor said she was stable, oh why, why, why?" She began to sob uncontrollably.

"What?" David wondered. "Um, ma'am, hello? Hello?"

"Yes?" came a tear-muffled voice.

"I may have my information confused. I'm sorry if I mistakenly alarmed you, ma'am. I thought you just told JP that Sharon had died."

"Oh, thank God, thank God!" Sharon's mom quickly uttered. "No, honey, I told him that she was in a terrible accident and that she was in the hospital, and that her car is dead, totaled, laid to rest, kaput."

"Oh, I get it now."

"I told Jean Paul he needs to get a new phone; it never has a good signal. Oh, my goodness sweetie, I can't believe I just lost it like that. I am just a wreck, my emotions have just been all over the place with Sharon in the hospital, and things are just so tough at home, and… how old did you say you were?"

"I'm sixteen."

"Oh, really? 'Cause you sound so much older and mature, and strong, and…"

David cut her off, "Well, let me find JP before he does something crazy."

"Yeah, you do that, honey. You know he's a cutter, especially when he's stressed. Oh, and tell Jean Paul that Sharon is in room 307 at the hospital, and the number is 368-1344. Oops, silly me, that's my number. But you can keep it if you ever need it."

"Oookay then, thanks. Hey, uh, this phone is breaking up again, so, uh, gotta go, bye!"

David shook his head, "Man, that woman is a trip. Wonder what she meant by JP is a cutter?"

David reached in JP's bag for the handgun. He took it out, removed the clip, and emptied the bullets. He replaced the empty clip back inside the gun, and hid the bullets in his pocket to throw away, and then set out to find JP.

As he was walking, David heard a voice sing out, "Hey, Musiq Soulchild."

He looked up to find Michal driving a cherry red, drop top BMW with peanut butter interior.

"You need a ride?" she called.

David turned his back and acted like he was picking something up off the ground and did the quick undercover smell check — (breath, underarms, and cologne). He was straight.

Standing back up, he looked over at her and replied, "Uh yeah, I kinda do."

"Well, get in," she motioned. "Where are you headed?"

"Trying to find my boy, JP."

"Oh? Where is he?"

"Um, if I knew that I wouldn't be trying to find him."

"Oh, okay, I see you got jokes. Do you want me to kick you out of my car?"

"See, I was just playin, Ma."

Michal turned to look at David, "Ma?"

"Yeah, Ma. It's a little phrase we use on the east coast when talking to fine sistas that got it goin on." David grinned, "No, but seriously, the last I saw him he was headed east of here."

Michal started to smile, but quickly concealed it before David noticed.

"Well, my name is Michal, and you can call me by that."

"Okay, Michal, I think your name is kinda cute." Suddenly shooting up straight in his seat, he pointed, "Hold up, there goes JP right there in front of the hospital."

Michal pulled into the hospital front parking lot. JP was sitting on an outside bench with his face buried in his hands, visibly weeping.

Michal asked, "Why is he crying?"

"Long story. Give me a minute."

David got out of the BMW and hurried over to his friend. He lightly touched his shoulder, "JP…"

"Leave me alone," JP muttered. Then he looked up and cried, "Yo Dave, I feel like my heart has shattered into a million pieces, man!"

JP reached up and grabbed David's face in his hands, looking him square in the eyes, "Dave, if you love someone, tell them. Don't hide it in the deep recesses of pride and ego. Show your true feelings, express yourself. Sharon made me want to run naked in a field of tulips and frolick in the dew of the dawn, but I had to be Mr. Freak and do her mom. Why, man, why?"

"JP…"

"It's horrible Dave; I'll never get the chance to make this right, now!"

"JP!" David broke JP's hands from his face and held his wrists, "JP, listen to me, man, Sharon is alive."

"What?"

David held tight to JP's wrists to keep him from falling over from the apparent shock.

"Sharon is alive," David repeated

"She's alive?" JP squeaked.

"Yes, she's alive."

JP leapt to his feet, bear hugging David and shouting, "She's alive! She's alive! I love you, man!" JP impulsively kissed David on the cheek.

"Yuck!" David pushed JP away, wiping at his cheek.

"Do you two need a room or something?" Michal broke in.

David looked annoyed, "Ha ha, very funny, Michal."

"Just checking," she replied.

JP had finally come to himself. Looking over at Michal, he asked, "Um, did you hear what I was saying?"

"Nah, I didn't hear anything about you frolicking naked in a field of tulips, nope sure didn't," she grinned.

JP looked from Michal to David. Both were trying hard not to laugh, but it was obvious. Michal's shoulders were shaking as she swallowed against the giggles that threatened release, and David kept his fist pressed against his lips.

JP glared at them, "Well, it takes a very secure man to frolic. You know what, forget ya'll!" He held up three fingers and said, "Read between the lines," causing David and Michal to laugh that much harder.

David said, "Well, now that you are done frolicking, Sharon is in room 307. I'll catch up with you later man."

"Cool, and, hey Dave, thanks for everything, man."

David paused as he felt the weight of JP's sincerity, and replied with conviction, "No problem, JP, that's what friends are for."

David and Michal got back in her car and drove off. They went by the coffee shop and small talked about Orange County over a couple of iced lattes, then Michal suggested they drive out to the coastline.

They were enjoying an easy conversation during the drive until Michal said, "Your boy's got issues, David."

David immediately went on the defensive, "Yeah, well, who doesn't? Everyone has something they have to deal with, some more than others."

Michal continued, not realizing she was pushing David's buttons, "Yeah, but he's kinda crazy and weird. And what was he wearing?"

David turned to glare at Michal, "What do you mean by that?"

"I'm just saying…"

"What are you saying, Michal? Yo, everyone out here thinks they know people just from their appearance. Judging folks based on what designer they are wearing, that's just messed up! If you're gonna judge my boy after spending two minutes with him, then you're even more arrogant and self-centered than people say you are."

"David, I didn't mean…"

"Ahhhh, save it. Let me out! I don't want to bring down the value of your car 'cause I don't have the same status or money you have."

Michal shrieked, "EXCUSE ME?!"

"Grow up Michal, with your high society, no manners, spoiled brat attitude."

"Wait a minute!" Michal brought the car to a screeching halt. "Who do you think you are that you think you can talk to me like that?"

"Who do you think you are that I can't? I'm out, Your Highness."

David jumped out of the car and bounced off without even bothering to close the door. Michal, fuming with anger, reached over and slammed the door shut. Without another word, she sped off, tires squealing.

## Chapter 9
# From Bad to Worse

David decided to go home and get ready for work and let off some steam. Two hours later, David reached the front door of Luas Corp and tried to use his security badge, but access was denied. He tried five more times, but it was still denied. Finally, the security guard came out to talk with David.

"Yo, Tony my badge is trippin', can you let me in?"

"Sorry, David, I can't do that."

"What? Are you serious? Quit playin' man, I got a lot of work to do."

"I'm not playing, Dave. Apparently you don't work here anymore."

"What? No way! Yo, my rooms are always done to perfection, and I'm never late, and…"

Tony cut him off, "Dave, listen to me, it has nothing to do with your work. I think you pissed somebody off in the higher-ups."

"This is crazy! This is absolutely crazy!" David shouted. "I don't even know none of them dudes, never seen them or talked to them!"

"Easy dawg, I'm your friend. Don't kill the messenger. I don't know what to tell you, but somebody has it out for you."

David quickly composed himself, "Sorry man, what do I need to do?"

"Listen, usually they mail your last check to you, which can take up to an extra week or so. But, come back in two weeks and I'll have it here for you personally."

"Sure. Hey, thanks Tony, I appreciate that."

"No problem, you my dawg; and if I hear anything I'll let you know."

David forced a smile, "Cool."

Tony gave David a sympathetic look, "Keep your head up, things will get better. Peace."

David was so frustrated, he was not sure what to do. Suddenly, his phone signaled a new text.

It was JP. "D where r u @?" it read.

David hit him back, "Go'n home."

"Meet u there."

"Cool."

JP and David met at the house. David was furious. He told JP about what happened with Michal and then what happened at his job. "I can't believe this day started out so great and turned out so terrible. Dang!"

"First of all, I don't care what Michal says about me or my mama," JP said, "it's Michal! She is fine and rich, and fine and sexy, and did I mention she is fine?"

"JP, I don't care how fine she is. She ain't all that to think that folks should bend over backwards for her stuck up behind! Ask me if I care about her money or her car. I thought she was cool, but she is a witch.

JP laughed.

"Dawg, why are you laughing? It ain't funny."

"Yeah, it is."

"No, it isn't!"

"Yes, it is."

"No, it ain't!"

"Yes, yes it is," JP insisted, still laughing.

"Okay, you tell me why you think this is sooo hilarious."

"Because, you are in love with this girl and you don't even know it. And, because she is feeling the same way."

"Huh? How do you figure?" David asked, confused.

"Dude, are you really as dumb as you look right now? Why do you think you got fired?"

"I have no idea. And what does that have to do with Michal? Stay on task, man, you are so scatterbrained sometimes."

"Fool, shut-up! Sit your tail down and maybe you can learn something. The two situations are one in the same, man. You got fired because you pissed Michal off, and her daddy owns Luas Corp. If Michal is mad, then daddy is going to fix it, and he sure fixed you!"

"What? How did she even know I worked there?"

"She's been checkin' a brotha out!"

"So Michal is heir to the throne of Luas Corp?"

"Not exactly, her brother Jonathan is next in line. But, he is away in school right now. He actually should be graduating in like, two weeks, and becoming the senior vice-president of Luas Corp. Yeah, there is supposed to be a huge party — everybody is buzzing about. I'm surprised you haven't heard anything about it. It's gonna be a big black tie gala affair. I'm trying to get my hands on some tickets!"

"So this chick got me fired?" David felt a new rush of energy, ready to meet Michal's unspoken challenge. "Okay, well two can play that game."

"What are you going to do?"

"Someone told me a long time ago the best revenge is success. It's time for my A-game."

"Fool, you ain't got *no* game," JP laughed.

"I know, but she doesn't know that. Hey, what happened with Sharon?"

"It's all good. She's scratched up pretty good, but when she woke up and she saw me there with flowers and a teddy bear, she couldn't help but smile. She took me back."

"Just like that?"

"Whose side are you on, Dave? I thought you would be happy for me."

"I am, but I'm just surprised she really took you back with just some flowers and a teddy bear. I know you're good, but not that good. What really happened?"

"Okay, okay! I kinda broke down in front of her. When I got there, she looked so weak and helpless, and she was all bandaged up. I couldn't see her face. I held her hand, and began to pray."

David broke in, surprised, "You were praying?"

"Dude, do you want to hear this or not? And yes, I do know how to pray, sort of. So, while I was praying, it really hit me how much she really means to me. I couldn't hold back the tears, and I apologized and begged for her forgiveness and told her how much I love her."

"You did what?"

"Yeah man, I told her how much I love her, and how honored I was to know her. The funny thing was, I was so sincere; I didn't have to think of things to say. Then her eyes opened and…" JP broke off, staring down at his feet.

"What, what?" David urged.

"It wasn't Sharon, it was her roommate! Sharon was in the bathroom, and when she came out, she said, 'Still flirting with other women, I see!' I was speechless. Then she walked over to me and hugged me and kissed me and said, 'I heard everything, and I forgive you. I love you too and I miss you.' She said she has missed me for a long time and has been praying for me."

"Wow!" David was amazed, "So then what happened?"

"I snuck her in some real food from Chick-fil-A, her favorite restaurant, because that hospital food is just plain nasty."

"Oh yeah, she's a keeper. She has great taste in food, Chick-fil-A, baby!"

"Yeah, I knew you would like that. Then we talked until visiting hours were over. She is looking forward to meeting you, and she is happy about our new partnership. She thinks you are a good influence on me. So, we are just going to take it one day at a time. Oh, and I'm forbidden to be around her mother alone."

"Yeah, that might be for the best. Hey, Sharon's mom said something about you being a cutter. What's that?"

"She did?"

"Yeah, she did. I didn't know what she was talking about. I thought it was like a secret society or something."

JP laughed, "I never really thought of it like that, but I guess you could call it that. Most of us that cut do it in secret."

"Cut what?"

"Ourselves, Dave, we cut ourselves."

David stiffened and eyed JP warily.

"Don't speak, just listen," said JP. "There are tons of people around the world that engage in self-injury, I just choose to cut. I told you I have been through a lot with my family, and as a young kid I felt powerless and didn't know how to deal with the pain. I found that cutting seemed to make me feel better, but in the long run it has actually caused me more pain, including hospital visits because I have cut too deep before. I almost died a couple of times. I know it seems like living in Orange County should be an amazing life, but material things don't take away pain. Substances may numb it for it a while, but it comes back stronger and stronger.

The other day you asked me about the bandage on my wrist. I said it was a burn, but actually, I had cut too deep. My dad and I had gotten into a bad fight, and he proceeded to cuss me and my mother out. I was ready to kill him, but I just swallowed that anger and all I knew to do was to cut. But, I have been listening to Pastor Nate and I have been praying more and working on my music, trying to channel my emotions into a positive way, you know?"

"Wow, man, I had no idea," David said softly.

"Most people don't. They just sit on the sidelines, judge, and assume. At least you had the balls to ask."

"No man, I feel you. I know what it's like to hurt and not know how to fix it. Music and computers — well hacking — has always been a great outlet for me — it's been my therapy. The ability to create a sound or a song, to say what I want to say, how I want to say it without anyone's permission; it's like a different type of freedom. Hacking enabled and challenged me to learn how to get around boundaries and obstacles set up to keep me confined in a place where people wanted me to stay. I know hackers that really hurt people or do some pretty horrible things; that was never my thing. I just like to be able to figure stuff out and conquer things. I know that might sound crazy, but it has kinda helped me in life, especially dealing with my mom's death. She would always say, 'Look for the solution, there can't be a problem without a solution. Don't let the problem conquer you, find the answer.' Maybe, that's what we should be doing."

"Hacking? I don't know how to..."

"No, no JP, not hacking; but this music thing for real. I mean, you are good at production and you've got some skills. Together I know we can make it happen and it could help us find some solution and peace in our lives. I mean, it's worth a try."

"Oh yeah, that reminds me, I almost forgot. I told Sharon about our financial situation."

"*Our* financial situation? I'm the one that got fired JP."

"Well, you know, I have been kinda getting convinted about the shady business dealings."

"Convinted?" David asked, confused.

"Yeah, convinted.  That's what Pastor Nate always says."

David shook his head and smiled, "I think you mean convicted."

"Whatever, Einstein.  Sharon said that she has been booking for this club in LA on the weekends; it's this crazy open mic spot.  Winner takes home a grand, but you can also sell your cd's as well.  And, if you are good, you can get on as regulars."

"For real?" David paused, his face clouded with a look of concern.

"What?  What's wrong?"

"Nothing, I was just thinking."

"Thinking?  Thinking about what?  If you're not with it, we can do something else."

"No, no, I'm with it.  I don't know, it just seems like things are changing so rapidly in my life, and I should be worried or concerned, but I'm actually at peace.  I mean, I have a sense that everything is going to work out better than just okay.  Matter of fact, I think this is just the beginning for us.  Like maybe we need to get ready and hone our skills."

# Chapter 10
# The Hook-Up

During the next six weeks, David and JP were constantly working on their music, putting singles together for their mixtapes. Their sound and chemistry on stage was improving at an accelerated rate. Sharon had gotten them some good opportunities at a few open mic spots around the city and they were creating a buzz. David was hitting the gym hard morning and night, before and after school, pushing up the weights and getting ripped. He was focused on getting prepared for any and every opportunity that was to come his way.

One rainy evening, after leaving the gym, he saw a truck hydroplane off the road and landed in a small road construction trench. David rushed over to see if the driver was okay. He could tell that the back tire was stuck and would need to be pushed out of the mud. When the driver got out, David realized that it was the same guy, the ring leader, that had beat him up on his first day of school, the same one David had knocked out days later during lunch. David's first reaction was to turn around and leave, but he knew he had to turn the other cheek and help this guy out.

"Get back in the truck," David motioned, "and I'll push."

David pushed while the driver floored the gas, causing the tires to spin and sling mud all over David.

Still, David pushed and pushed until the truck gave way and pulled out of the ditch. David straightened, wiping futilely at the mud, and watched as the truck just drove away. The driver never once offered David a word or wave of appreciation.

"Figures," David muttered, shaking his head. Looking down, he saw that he had dropped his pre-paid cell phone in a mud puddle. He hollered, "Son of a…"

"Excuse me, young man," a voice broke in. "Can you help an old lady with her bags?" David had not noticed the elderly woman when she approached. She was short and stout, and seemed to be struggling with a couple of grocery bags in her hand.

"Umm, sure ma'am." Taken off guard, but still glad to help, David reached for her bags.

"Thank you, son," she replied.

David carried the lady's bags across the street and just down the block.

"This is far enough, son, I can manage them the rest of the way," she told David.

"Are you sure? I don't mind," David replied.

Reaching for her bags, the elderly woman smiled at David, "Don't you let things get to you, young man. Life is always subject to change, and I have a feeling that the circumstances in your life are about to turn around for you."

"Thank you, ma'am." David welcomed the kind words, as they seemed to blanket him with a peace he so needed. It was odd, but he felt compelled to believe her.

David turned to head home, but then turned back in the woman's direction, intending to ask her name. However, she was gone!

"Where did she go so fast?" David wondered.

David stopped a passerby and asked if he saw where the lady had gone.

"I didn't see anybody but you," the man replied.

"That's strange," David thought as he headed home. "I wonder if… nah, no way."

———◆———

At home, David went to grab a drink from the fridge when he saw a note posted there for him:

"David,

Linda, myself and the boys went to the movies. There's pizza in the fridge, and your friend, JP, dropped off a package for you. It's on the kitchen table.

See you later,

Mr. King"

David went downstairs and got cleaned up, then came back up and popped the pizza in the microwave. While it was heating, he grabbed the package off the table. Inside, he found a black box for bootlegging free cable TV.

"Ohhh, yeah!" David started dancing around the kitchen, "We got all the channels, baby!"

The microwave dinged, and David reached in and grabbed the plate, shoving a piece of piping hot pizza in his mouth without thinking.

"OOOOOuch! Hot! Hot! Hot!" David shouted. Pizza still in hand, David ran for the sink, spewing cheese and tomato sauce, when he tripped over a chair.

There was a knock at the back door, and without giving David a chance to respond, JP strolled in, eyes wide, taking in the scene.

David was sprawled across the floor, pizza toppings splayed across his face and shirt, empty plate laying beside his head.

"Dude, you are wasted!" accused JP.

"No, I'm not"

"Uh, yes you are."

"NO, I'm not!"

"YES, you are!"

"NO, I'M NOT" David shouted.

"Okay," JP whispered under his breath, "yes, you are."

"JP, what do you want?" David growled, slowly pulling himself up from the floor.

JP offered his hand to help, and asked, "Dude, did you see my surprise, the black box? I scored it last night; had a little gambling action going on."

"I told you about all that gambling. I thought you said you quit? You're gonna find your head in a vice or something one day."

"Dave, you've been watching too much 'Casino.' Did you hook it up yet?"

David thought to himself, "'Casino,' I love that movie!" To JP, he replied, "No, not yet. How 'bout you hook it up for me and make yourself useful."

"You ain't said nothing but a word. Besides, I got another surprise for you."

"What now, JP?" David sighed.

"Oh, you'll see." JP's eyes were wild, looking as if he just drank a whole case of Red Bull.

They went downstairs, and JP shooed David out of the room while he hooked the cable up. David went in the bathroom and got cleaned up for the second time that day, while waiting for JP. When he was done, JP called David back into the room.

"A'ight, who's your boy? Say it!"

"JP, just turn the dang thing on."

"And a one, and a two and a three, what the…?"

"Uh, JP, it might help if you plug in the power cord," David smirked, swinging the end of the power cord in his hand.

JP grinned sheepishly, "Oh, yeah. My bad, son!"

As he handed JP the cord, David reminded him, "JP, I told you before, you need to just stick with 'dude.'"

"Lights camera, actioooooon!" JP waived a few circles in the air with his hands to add to the dramatic flair.

As the TV screen lit up, David and JP stood staring, mouths agape, at the big screen in awe. At that moment, both would have sworn to an angelic choir singing hallelujahs in the distance.

After several moments passed, JP finally spoke, a single tear streaming down his cheek, "Wow, this is such a beautiful thing. I love you man."

Pointing the remote at the TV, JP started flipping through the channels — seemingly endless channels. JP settled on one of the movie channels playing 'Saving Private Ryan.' The opening scene unfolded on the big screen, almost lifelike.

"Time for my surprise," JP whispered.

JP hit a button on the remote, and suddenly the room exploded with gunshot noises. David instinctively hit the floor like the target of a drive by.

"What the heck is that?" shouted David, embarrassed and overwhelmed.

"Surround sound, baby!" JP shouted back in order to be heard. "My boy works at Best Buy and he gave me the hook up."

JP continued cruising the channels, ESPN, Food Network, FOX, Showtime, BET… he landed on an adult channel and paused. David looked over at JP who was staring at the TV screen as if he were in a trance. "Ooooooh, give it to me, daddy," a woman's voice purred through the speakers.

"JP!"

"What?" JP tried to look innocent.

"Turn the channel, you pervert."

"Oh sorry," JP sighed, as he reluctantly began channel surfing again.

He was just flipping through the locals when David said, "Wait a minute, go back."

"That's what I'm talking about!" JP grinned.

"No, go back to the local OCC News."

"Oh, maaan," JP whined.

"JP, hurry up, I saw something," David urged.

"Yeah, I saw something too," JP muttered.

Back on the local channel, headlines were flashing across the screen, "Goliath Strikes Again!"

"There has been a string of cyber crimes," announced a male reporter from the news desk. "A virus called 'Goliath' has been uploaded to major corporations' computer systems, shutting down all computer activities and causing companies to lose billions of dollars until they pay a high ransom. Initially, everyone thought it was just a prank, until three major businesses went bankrupt due to this virus. According to the report, this virus is untraceable and the hacker is still unknown. Most companies are just paying the ransom."

"Oh man, that's crazy!" said JP.

With a look of intrigue, David never looked away from the screen as he replied, "Man, I know I could fix this problem."

# Chapter 11
# Lions, Tigers, Bears And Leon?

"What?" JP shot David a skeptical look. "Come on, Dave. I know you are good at the computer thing, but if no one else can stop this guy, what makes you think you can?"

"JP, when I was in Brooklyn, I was one of the best hackers in the region. My crew and I had things on lock. We had a network running, using NYU's network server, their mainframe. We used to create viruses just for the fun of it, and we also had anti-virus programs to combat other hackers from taking us out. Well, long story short, my crew was making a lot of money. We were changing grades for people, giving test answers before exams.

We had dirt on executives and we were trading everything you could think of; we even had online gambling. It was crazy! We were all still in junior high and high school, and nobody could trace it back to us until..." David paused for effect.

"Until what?" JP asked, obviously intrigued.

"One of my guys in the crew had a sister that attended NYU. He actually looked older and he had some game. He was the one that made the initial contact. He met this work study student named Tiffany that was working in the executive office as an assistant to the administrative assistant for admissions. She was a nice girl, but not too secure in who she was, so he flirted with her, acting like he was a student on work study for the IT department at NYU."

"IT department?" JP asked, confused.

"The department that handles the maintenance for all the computers on campus," David explained. "He was able to get all the info we needed on the execs, and even some key passwords. Well, the plan was for him to just be nice, get the info and be out. But she started liking him, and they ended up having a romantic relationship. His ego wouldn't let it go 'cause he was a high school student pulling an older woman. You should know all about that, JP."

"Oh yes! 'Girls Gone Wild College Edition!' Don't I kn…"

"JP! Stay focused."

"Sorry, Dave."

"Anyway, the girl invited him to this party one of the Black Greek Fraternities was throwing. So this fool went. Okay, I ain't going to lie, we all went, not thinking about the fact that his sister was in a sorority and she would be there. We had our fake IDs and everything. It was dark inside the party, so no one could really see how old we were. The party was off the hook! There were honeys everywhere. I was dancing with all kinds of girls: big girls, skinny girls, cute girls, ugly girls, I didn't care. So we were all just doing our thing, until my boy started grinding all up on this other girl and Tiffany got pissed.

She slapped the mess out of him and asked, 'Samson' — that was his alias, his real name is Jamal — 'why are you all up on this ho!?' The girl he was dancing with stopped and rolled her neck, 'B, I ain't no HO, but your MAMA is!'

"It was all over then. The crowd erupted in a chorus of 'Oooooo's.' Somebody hollered, 'Can't we all just get along?' It looked like a fight was about to break out when my boy's sister recognized him and said, 'Jamal Lamont Parker, what are you doing here?'

"Then Tiffany pipes up, 'His name is Samson!'

"Jamal's sister turned on her, waiving her index finger, 'This is my brother, little girl, and he is only sixteen-years-old, so you'd better get somewhere before I beat you down for robbing the cradle!' Jamal's sister grabbed Jamal by the ear and escorted him, and us, out of that party. Tiffany never spoke to Jamal again."

"Daaang!!!" JP crowed. David noticed JP had made his way to the couch, munching on a mystery bag of popcorn that seemed to have appeared from nowhere, obviously engrossed — and entertained. "And? Come on, what happened next?"

"Well, Monday morning we all got busted! Jamal conveniently failed to tell us that he had told Tiffany all about our activities one night after she had put it on him. They pulled us into the office and threatened to call the police if we didn't tell them everything. Now, here's where it gets interesting," David raised his brows, "I don't know if you remember, but a few years ago there were like five college presidents from major universities that were fired because of embezzlement."

"I think I remember something like that," said JP.

"Well, there was a virus called 'The Bear.' It was nasty! It would basically snatch confidential information and then print it out on every printer connected to the network. Well, this virus printed out some bank statements along with some very sensitive information exposing illegal activity, which caused the firing of a number of prominent men. They are lucky that they didn't get some serious jail time. But, because of the possibility of evidence contamination, they were just slapped hard on the wrist. Anyway, the president of NYU was afraid that something like that could happen at his school. Actually, he thought that we were the creators of The Bear virus! It took a lot of convincing to plead our case and prove that we were not the ones.

So, long story short, he hired us to develop a security program and virus-fix to protect them against any such virus. We developed a program called 'Slingshot,' an anti-virus program that could take any virus known or unknown, quarantine it, and then sling it back to the originator. This thing was hot! It stopped The Bear virus right in its tracks. The University was more than appeased, and agreed not to turn us in to the authorities in exchange for the program. In the end, we had to disband our network."

"Oh," David continued, "when Jamal's mom found out, she went off; cut off his internet, took his computer for a year, and grounded him for about six months. His mama didn't play, and neither did mine. It felt like forever before I had my own computer again!"

"Wow!" whistled JP.

"Yeah, and believe it or not, man, I've dealt with even worse viruses since then. I was attacked by this hacker called 'Mufasa,' guess he thought he was the king of the jungle or something. He had this virus called 'Leo' that would hack into your email files and send you back a response to an email you had sent someone. As soon as you opened it, it would take full control over your computer. It would then send viruses to all your contacts in your contact list using your email address, instituting a chain reaction."

"So how did you stop it?" asked JP.

"Well, when I found out what was going on, I called Jamal, who was still grounded. Because he was on punishment, his computer wasn't infected. So we upgraded Slingshot to not only sling the virus back to its origin, but we added a little something to it, like a bomb of sorts. That thing was nasty! If it were a bullet, it would be a hollow point. Most 'bombs' just crash the hard drive, but we made it so that not only would it crash the hard drive, but it would turn off the exhaust fan and force the computer to run so fast it would overheat and actually melt everything on the inside of the computer itself, even if you unplugged it." David paused and chuckled for effect, "Let's just say Leo never bothered us again."

"Oh, that's just mean!" JP quipped with admiration.

"Hey, you sow the wind, you reap the whirlwind, baby!" David grinned.

"So what are you going to do?"

"Well, I need to reconstruct the anti-virus. When my mom died and I moved out here, I was kinda in a daze; everything happened so fast. I left everything in Brooklyn because I wanted to start over and just forget my past, well, the pain of the past."

"How long is it going to take for you to reconstruct this anti-virus?"

"Not long, maybe about a week or so. I need to get my hands on a laptop."

"Don't worry about it, I got you covered," JP waived his hand in a gesture of dismissal.

"What do you mean, you got it covered?"

"Dave, ask me no questions, I'll tell you no lies."

"JP? I thought you were leaving the shady business deals behind!"

"See, now you just hurt my feelings," JP feigned mock hurt. "I told you, don't worry about it. I'll see you in a couple of days with the hottest laptop you can imagine."

Two days later, JP produced the laptop as promised.

"JP, what kind of laptop is this?"

"Its a 'Leon,'" JP answered matter-of-factly.

"A what? A Leon?" David turned the laptop this way and that, trying to figure out what off-brand, piece of computer JP was trying to pawn on him.

"Yeah, a Leon. It's hot right?"

"Hot? I don't even know what this is! I thought you were going to bring me something name brand, or at least recognizable. I mean, what kind of operating system is this? What kind of laptop is a Leon?"

JP stopped David with a hard look, "Why don't you turn it on and see for yourself? My boy Leon builds them, so we call it 'Leon.' Why don't you just trust me for once in your life? Dang!"

David hit the power button, and it was on! The Leon was the fastest computer David had ever seen, lightning fast! Ten minutes later, David told JP, "This is a work of art, man! I have never seen a computer this fast or this quiet. It's incredible!"

"Yeah, I know. I told you I would deliver. You know, Dave, I may look like I'm dumb, but I'm not stupid. I have connects you wouldn't believe. Don't let my looks fool you; I have a global swag, and if we're going to be partners, friends, or homies, you need to recognize and respect your boy. There are some guys ready to rock with you Dave, but they ain't from the right side of the tracks, yet they have more talent, smarts, and ambition than that other side of the tracks could ever have. Everything isn't always what it seems."

David was taken aback. He had never heard JP come at him like that before.

"My bad, JP. I didn't mean to disrespect you or your boy. I have just never seen anything like this before. And, believe me, I wasn't born with a silver spoon in my mouth. My mom busted her butt so I could learn and have the possibility of something better. Anyway, who does your boy work for?"

JP grinned, "Nobody right now. He was trying to work for Luas Corp, but he has a record and doesn't fit into the corporate America model. So, he's been building computers as a side hustle."

"This kid could change the technology game if he gets the right backing. Well, tell your boy anything I can do to help, I am more than willing."

JP laughed, "Yeah, I know. He's just like us, waiting on his break. I've already

set a plan into motion for a business partnership between him and us."

"You did what?!"

"Breathe Dave, breathe. You've gotta
seize the moment. So I set up a little business venture, where he builds these computers and we get them into the right
markets, and everybody gets paid. And
we all know that you need to be making
some money right about now."

"JP, man, if this laptop wasn't so hot, it
would be me and you — and mostly me;
but I don't have time for that right now. I
gotta get to work building the toughest
anti-virus program you have ever seen!"

## Chapter 12
# Let the Games Begin

The long hours David had been spending at the gym were finally showing signs of paying off. Late one evening, he was finishing his workout with a round of bench presses, having added extra weights to further challenge his growing muscles. As he counted off reps, "seven... eight," he grunted and mumbled, "That's enough for today."

A familiar voice approached, "Come on man, you can do more than that."

"Seriously?" David sighed, as he looked up to see the same guy, the 'ring leader' of the varsity Lacrosse team he had had the run ins with at school, not to mention the truck in the mud incident. Rolling his eyes, David said, "Come on man, not today. I'm just trying to finish my workout and be out. I don't want any trouble."

"Well, work out then. You have at least three more reps in you. I'll spot you."

David eyed him warily as he reluctantly laid back on the bench and pushed the barbell, "nine... ten..." David's arms trembled as he struggled with the next press, "elev... oof!" David's arms gave out beneath the strain. Quickly, David's questionable spotter caught the bar and lifted it back into its cradle.

"See, doesn't that feel better?"

"Man, I feel like my chest is about to jump out of my skin," David wheezed, gasping to catch his breath.

"You have to push yourself. Look, I know you're wondering why I am here."

"The thought did cross my mind."

"Well, I just wanted to say thanks about the other day with the truck. I'm not good at apologies, so I'm not going to say I'm sorry. But I do appreciate you helping me out when I know I didn't deserve it. That wasn't my truck. I kinda borrowed it on a dare, and I had to get it back before anyone knew it was missing. So, I guess you could say that you saved my, well, you know."

"No problem," David nodded. "I just don't want any more beef between us."

"You got it, man. Actually, you don't have to worry about that anymore. Matter of fact, if anyone messes with you, it will be like they're messing with me."

"Now this is a twist," David thought, but he just nodded again in silent agreement.

"By the way," he continued, "I see you're trying to bulk up. My dad owns a health and nutrition shop. Whatever you need man, I'll hook you up. Cool?"

"Cool."

Out of the corner of his eye, David saw Michal walking by. It was the first time he had seen her since he had been fired about six weeks before.

"Yo man, what is your name anyway?"

"Its Craig James, actually it's Uriah Craig James, but my friends call me Big C."

"Thanks man, I'll catch you later. Right now, I gotta run and catch up with this trifling girl."

David ran out the gym, shirtless and dripping with sweat, his chest still pumped from that last set of reps.

"Michal... Michal!" he called.

Michal turned around, and when she saw David's broad bare chest glistening with sweat, her heart fluttered. She tried to be discreet with her admiration, but David caught her eyes wandering over his physique.

"So, you got a brother fired? Is that how you deal with conflict?" David challenged.

"I don't know what you are talking about," Michal looked away as she denied his accusation.

"Come on Michal, let's be real. You saw an attractive, talented, sexy brother that wasn't going to let you get away with being spoiled and rude, and you couldn't handle that." David half smiled as he verbally pushed Michal, but he pushed a little too hard, for she flew back at him.

"What? You arrogant... first of all I'm not spoiled! And yes, you have some talent in a Sesame Street talent search type of a way, but attractive and sexy? I have had cuter guys approach me at the annual YMCA Thanksgiving charity event in the city, and they were homeless!" Then, there was silence.

David recovered with some swag of his own, "Oh it's like that? So now you're saying I don't have talent and I'm not cute. So why is it your eyes keep wandering downward towards my six pack? If you want to touch, all you have to do is ask." At that moment David took Michal's hand and pressed it across his stomach. Michal could feel the definition of each abdominal muscle while David sucked in to hold his stomach tight. The tension between them sparked momentarily as Michal allowed her hand to caress his mid-section, fingers tracing the ripples of his muscles. Her eyes slipped shut and she took an involuntary sharp intake of breath. David smiled, he had her right where he wanted her, but then Michal caught herself.

Snapping her eyes open and jerking back her hand, she snipped, "I don't have time for this, I've gotta go. Keep working out David, maybe by next year you will be up to Snoop Dogg's size."

Michal snatched the towel from David's shoulder, wiped the sweat off her hand, then threw the towel back at him and stormed off.

"Whatever!" David shouted after her. To himself, he growled, "Ugh, I can't stand that girl!" Suddenly distracted, he stopped, "What is this?" David stooped down to pick up a loose flyer off the ground. It read, "School Play — Last Day for Auditions." Michal had dropped it.

"Interesting," David mused. "Hmm, today is the last day to audition. Why not? But I need to hurry up if I'm going to make it."

David rushed to shower and get changed, then ran all the way to the school's auditorium. He was still late for the auditions, and had no idea what he would have to do, but he had made up his mind that some way or other he was going to get into the play so he could 'teach Michal a lesson' and show her that he was indeed talented.

When he finally made it to the auditorium, he was shocked to see that there was a long line of kids waiting to audition. You would have thought that they were casting for a major film or something. There were kids rehearsing their scales, and many were carrying headshots, while others wore scarves and sipped hot tea. David tried asking several of the students closest to him about what he would need to do or where to go, but the other kids either ignored him or pointed to their throats indicating that they were saving their voices for the audition. Frustrated, David broke out of line and ran to a pay phone to call JP; his pre-paid minutes had run out.

"Hello? Hello, JP?"

"Dave? Hold on, I don't have good reception here. Can you here me now?"

"Yeah, yo, I'm here at school about to audition for this play."

"Do you have headshots?"

"Headshots? Naw, I don't have any headshots, it's just a school play."

"So young, so green, so sad," JP's voice dripped with sarcasm. "Boy, you ain't in Kansas anymore, or wherever you're from. Out here, school plays are major productions. We have A&R people from record labels, and talent scouts who come to our school plays. It's a very big deal, dude."

"Dang!"

"Did you fill out your application?"

"No."

"Did you grease the student that's in charge of scheduling the auditions?"

"Nooo!" David's frustration was steadily rising.

"Have you picked a song, or do you know what part you are going to audition for, or…"

"No, no, and no! I just decided today to audition."

"Well mi amigo — that's 'dude' in Spanish — you are so not prepared, but luckily you have an agent that can get

126

you into places for a mere twenty percent commission."

"Agent?"

"Yes, fool, agent. Now do you want my help or not?"

"Yeah, but today is the last day."

"Don't worry about that. I'll have everything covered. You do realize that the play is not until next semester and you are going to have to give up a major portion of your summer break for this project?"

"Yeah, I understand all that," David replied.

"Well, just meet me at the spot at six. And get out of that crazy audition, we have a lot of work to do. "

"The spot?"

"Your house, fool! Peace! Oh yeah, and get some minutes for your phone; you on a pay phone is just plain embarrassing. Seriously!"

———◆———

When David finally arrived at the house, after getting his minutes sorted out, he found JP dressed in all black — black slacks, black dress shoes, black turtle neck, black sunglasses, and a black beret. David just shook his head in disbelief. He had never seen JP in anything but designer jeans and custom sneakers, and now he looked like an out of work artist. JP whipped out his flip camera and began filming.

"David, what is your motivation?" asked JP in a soft, raspy, 'Godfather' voice.

David was both annoyed and amused. "JP, stop playin'. I need to get into this play!"

"It's Jean Paul, and I can't just get you into this play without knowing your credentials."

"Come on, JP."

"It's Jean Paul," JP insisted.

"Quit playin', man. Okay, okay," David sighed, "quit playin', Jean Paul."

"That's better. Okay, here's the deal." JP put his camera away and continued, "I got you on the props crew."

"WHAT! Are you kidding me? You'd better be kidding me. I ain't doing no props!"

JP dropped the façade, "Look, this is the only way. You are on the stage props crew. Now, all you have to do is learn all your lines for the character you want to play, and be ready to step in when they drop out. Oh, and they will drop out," JP promised.

"What do you mean? How do you know?" David was confused.

"You know what, for a dude from New York, you're sounding like a little gur…"

David punched JP square in his chest before he could finish, and said, "I got your little girl."

"Dang man, I was just playin'. You need to leave them 'roids alone. It makes you all uptight and it makes your thingy small." JP continued to rub the spot on his chest where David had punched him.

"I'm not on steroids, JP."

"Leave the juice alone! Just say no. This is your brain on drugs, any questions?" JP doubled over with laughter at his own joke.

"JP!!!" David was quickly losing his patience.

"Look, just trust me, man. Sign up for the props stage crew and learn your lines. I will take care of the rest. Oh yeah, we'll work out my payment later."

"Payment?"

"Yeah, these are tough times, my friend, and nothing is free nowadays."

"JP, what are you going to do?"

JP resumed his 'Godfather' voice, "David, you should know by now, ask me no questions, I will tell you no lies. But when they ask you how or why you know the lines, tell them you had learned them for a play you were in in New York, got it? Dang you hit hard." JP was still rubbing his chest.

"Cool. I know, dawg. I've been working out and drinking milk."

"Yeah, milk mixed with muscle juice."

"Whatever," David rolled his eyes at JP while flexing his muscles and posing before the mirror.

## Chapter 13
# Dreams

That night, David couldn't stop thinking about Michal. He wondered how he could beat her at her own game by getting into the play. He knew that she liked him, she was just playing hard to get. The funny thing was, he was trying to convince himself that he didn't like her.

Instead of kicking it with JP, he decided to go to bed early. David fell asleep in front of the TV and began to dream. In his dream, he was standing outside in front of his house when it began to rain; but instead of raining water, it was raining money. There were so many one-hundred-dollar and fifty-dollar bills that they blanketed the yard like fallen leaves. David ran and grabbed a rake to gather the money into piles. Afterwards, he called JP and told him to come over quick. In an instant, JP appeared. He stared at the piles of money, then at David, then back at the money. With a loud whoop, he reached down and swept one of the piles up in his arms, and tossed it in the air. They both began to laugh, dance, and cry all at once. All their dreams were about to come true! JP ran and dove into another pile of money. There were millions of dollars in the yard. Suddenly, when David looked at JP, his clothes had changed. Gone were the jeans and hi-tops, now JP was dressed in a sharp Armani suit. David whistled and glanced down at himself. His clothes had changed too! Catching JP's eye, he raised his brows, and looked about. In the driveway were their dream cars, and the garage was stocked with state of the art studio equipment. JP grabbed his arm, pointing this way and that in wonder, when the loud crack of a single gunshot startled David awake.

David sat up and rubbed his eyes, "Man,that was some dream!"

He got up and fixed himself a glass of water before lying back down. With a yawn, he stretched and then drifted back to sleep. He began to dream again. This time, he was in the studio. The sound and energy was nothing short of magnetic! He looked up to find JP laying some of the hottest tracks he had ever heard. As he watched, he noticed JP whip out his tablet and smart phone and check his schedule – his boy had meetings set up with some of the hottest artists in the biz. Suddenly Sharon appeared, walked over to JP, circled her arms around his neck and kissed him soundly on the lips. JP smiled, gently unhooked her arms, and dropped down to plant a gentle kiss on her stomach, which was slightly protruding. JP appeared happier than David had ever seen him. Then it happened again, the crack of a single gunshot woke David up.

Dazed and still half-asleep, David shook his head to help clear it, got up, and turned off the TV. Next, he put on some soft, soothing music, and then went to the bathroom to wash his face and brush his teeth. Stripping down to his boxers, he grabbed a couple of blankets and and went back to sleep.

Just as he began to doze, he heard a loud knock at the door.

"Dang, JP! I gave you a key for a reason. I'm trying to sleep." Irritated, he snatched open the door.

"I'm not JP."

"Michal?" David wiped his eyes in disbelief.

Michal walked in, smelling like she had just stepped out of the shower, and the scent of her perfume filled the air. She had on a Chanel trench coat that tied at the waist and stiletto heels. She walked right past David into the house.

"What are you doing here Michal?"

She turned to glare at him, "I know what you are trying to do David, and it's not going to work. You and I come from two very different worlds. You can't handle a woman like me." Her expression softened as she continued, "Oh, you were very cute today, and I see you have been working out. But having a tight body is only the beginning. Many have failed trying to handle all this," she swept her arm emphatically down her side, indicating her stunning figure. Then suddenly, she pushed David down on the couch, straddled his lap, and tickled his neck with a rush of soft, sensual kisses. She breathed against his ear, "David, are you sure you are ready for this?"

David's voice was strained with desire, "Michal, I have wanted you from the time I laid eyes on you."

"Baby, I'm sorry I played so hard to get, but I have never had a guy give me butterflies and make me blush before."

David's fingers trembled as he reached for the tie on her raincoat. Quickly, he pulled it loose and ripped the raincoat open. He was astonished to find that she was only wearing a pair of boy shorts and a lacy bra underneath. Michal groaned as her kisses became more demanding, "Oh, David!"

"Shhh, not so loud, everyone is asleep upstairs," David whispered.

Michal called his name over and over, getting louder each time. David could hear the door to the upstairs opening and the sound of footsteps fast approaching. His heart began to race. Just as he pushed Michal off his lap, his phone rang, the volume somehow magnified. The caller ID read 'JP.' He quickly answered, "Hello? JP?"

"Dave, help me, please!" JP's panicked voice screeched through the phone.

David ran to the window and saw three black hearses slowly driving down the street.

A single gunshot went off. David awoke in a cold sweat.

RING Buzzzz RING! David eyes frantically darted around the now dark room.

RING Buzzzz RING! He realized his cell was going off, ringing and vibrating to indicate an incoming call. He reached for it, and a quick glance at the caller ID told him it was JP. RING Buzzz RING! Reluctantly, he answered the call. "Hello?" he said cautiously.

"Dave, help me, please?" JP's voice came through in a whisper.

David began to panic, "JP, are you okay? What's wrong man? Talk to me!"

"Ha, ha, ha!" JP laughed, "Gotcha dude!"

"Very funny. JP you play too much," David laughed back in an effort to disguise his lingering concern.

"Well, I couldn't sleep man. What are you doing?" JP asked.

"I couldn't sleep either. Been having these crazy dreams."

"For real? What were they about?"

"Ah, I don't feel like talking about it right now." David was still a little shaken by the dreams. He wondered what they could mean. The single gun shot, the three hearses, and JP calling on the phone asking for help; what was it all about? David had had strange dreams before, but none that were so vivid and seemed so real. "Yo, JP, I'll talk to you tomorrow."

"Okay Dave, peace."

# Chapter 14
# Sunday Morning

The Orange County Community Church had become part of David's regular Sunday morning routine. He really enjoyed it — except for the music. Each Sunday, David found himself sitting closer and closer to the front of the church, and actually taking notes from Pastor Nate's sermons. Pastor Nate saw something special in David and began investing time in him, informally mentoring him, sharing nuggets of wisdom during their talks. Despite the crazy dreams that had disturbed his sleep the night before, David woke up bright and early the following morning, and went on to church early.

When he arrived, he found Pastor Nate nervously pacing back and forth.

David asked, "Pastor Nate, are you okay?"

"No David, I'm not." Pastor Nate was visibly frustrated.

"What's wrong?"

"Well, the organist is on vacation."

David mutter beneath his breath, "That sounds like an answer to prayer to me."

"Pardon me?"

"Hope she's enjoying a well deserved rest," David quickly covered, not wanting to be disrespectful.

"Yes, of course. But, as I was saying, she's on vacation and her replacement just called in sick. Now I don't know what we'll do for music this morning."

"Don't worry about it, Pastor Nate. JP and I will take care of it."

"What? You and JP? Now David, I don't mean to belittle you, but are you two…"

"Trust me Pastor Nate," David cut him off and ran to the stage. Before Pastor Nate could respond, he realized the parishioners were quickly filing in. As he greeted the church, they automatically picked up their songbooks and flipped to an old hymn specified for that Sunday's opening worship music in the weekly program.

Several of the church members curiously eyed David as he turned the organ on and set one of the synthesizer keyboards on top. When he turned on the keyboard, there was a loud pop in the sound system, followed by a high pitched squeal that forced everyone to cover their ears.

A rush of worry deeply etched the pastor's face, and Mr. and Mrs. King stared on in horror. Mrs. King flushed with anger and embarrassment, muttering inaudibly beneath her breath, (which was good because what she was saying was not fit to be heard in a place of worship.) The King boys were laughing and pointing, and JP was struggling not to laugh himself.

David cleared his throat in the microphone, and nodded to Pastor Nate.

Not quite convinced, Pastor Nate turned toward the congregation and asked one of the church deacons to start the service with opening prayer. Afterwards, he instructed everyone to open their hymnals to page 214, and looked warily over toward David. With an exaggerated breath, he grudgingly nodded for David to begin.

David stretched his fingers, grinned in JP's direction, then closed his eyes and let his fingers dance across the keys. Suddenly, the dusty veil of an old humdrum fell away, and the church came alive! David played the same sweet hymns they were used to, but dressed them up with a feisty tempo.

At first, everyone just stared in shock. Then, an elderly lady began to sing. JP joined in from the back, and one-by-one, more joined them. By the third stanza, the entire church was singing, less Mrs. King.

Even the teenagers got caught up in the music. David opened his eyes to see the church clapping and bobbing their heads, and by the second song, they were on their feet.

JP broke for the front, and took a seat at the drums. The rhythm, and the spirit of worship it invoked, was amazing! Before turning the service over to Pastor Nate for the message, David paused the music and addressed the congregation.

"If you would, just close your eyes for this next song, and reflect on your life and how good God has been." With that, he broke into an easy rendition of 'Amazing Grace.' David's voice was golden, sweet as honey, as he sang. Hearts were tender and touched, ready to receive the Gospel message by the time Pastor Nate got up to preach.

And preach he did! Pastor Nate preached that morning like he had never preached before. After the service ended, the parishioners were buzzing about how it was the best service they had ever had. Several of the kids crowded David and JP, vocalizing their admiration. Someone suggested that they should start a band, and the rest agreed. A few even asked if they could join.

As the parishioners were leaving, David and JP met Pastor Nate at the front of the church, grinning from ear to ear. "I told you we could handle it Pastor Nate," David said proudly.

Pastor Nate was speechless. He patted them on their shoulders while giving an affirming nod, and he began to make his way to his office. As David and JP made their way to the exit, they were stopped by the voice of their Pastor. "Boys, thank you, thank you, thank you; you have no idea how much God used you today. I have been praying for a change in our church, and God used you — the both of you — to bring about that change. Your parents should be proud, and if they never say it to you, I am saying it for them. I am proud of you! Sometimes those closest to us can't see our value, many times we can't see our own value, but God sees and knows and has a way of honoring us in front of our haters if we will behave ourselves wisely. You are both valuable and significant. Never forget that."

It was what they both needed to hear. They were both struck speechless, yet motivated. They walked home in silence pondering what Pastor Nate had said.

By the next Sunday, Pastor Nate had cancelled the guest organist and placed David and JP over the new youth choir and band. It seemed like the church had doubled in size overnight. The energy inside was nothing short of incredible. Everyone seemed to have welcomed the much needed change. Sunday mornings at the Orange County Community Church were never the same.

# Chapter 15
# Mr. Luas

The following Friday, David went back to Luas Corp to pick up his final check. Tony, the head of security, had called just like he said he would. David showed up at three in the afternoon, per Tony's instructions, and waited at the front desk. David quickly observed that the office was a complete madhouse, as casual Fridays at Luas Corp tended to be.

Most of the staff had left early for the day, also typical of Fridays. Because of the resulting skeleton crew, Tony was fielding a rush of small emergencies for the executives while trying to get the security cameras fixed at the same time. David motioned to Tony for his check, and Tony nodded back, holding up a finger to let David know it would be just a minute.

While he waited, David heard a call come over the intercom that one of the closet doors was locked on the executive wing. Tony appeared to be overwhelmed, so David offered to help.

"That closet is on my old cleaning floor. I can unlock it if you want; I know exactly where it is."

Tony hesitated, then agreed, "Okay David, but come right back. I'm not supposed to let former employees in the building."

"What? Do you think I'm going to blow this place up just because I was fired without a cause?"

"That's not funny, David. Make sure you're right back. It's my job on the line if you do anything stupid!" Tony handed David the keys and a staff badge. David promised to be quick.

David made his way up to the executive wing. As he got off the elevator, he could hear someone yelling and cursing, saying how much he hated technology. David laughed as he walked down the hallway to the locked closet. He found the new cleaning guy there waiting for help.

David greeted him, "Hi, you couldn't get it open huh?

"No, my key doesn't work."

"Well, you just have to play with it a little bit, kinda jiggle it and... voila!" David smiled as the closet door popped open.

"Thanks man. I just started and I'm just getting the hang of things.

"That's cool, it will all fall into place for you," David assured him. "What's your name?"

"I'm Roger Coleman; started working here a couple of weeks ago."

"Really?"

"Yeah," replied Roger, avoiding eye contact. David noticed Roger seemed eager to get back to work, and did not appear to welcome distractions, so he excused himself.

"Cool, well Roger, I have to go. I hope everything works out for you."

David was headed back toward the elevator when an older man shouted for him from inside one of the offices.

"Hey, you with the keys, I've been waiting for you! I need some help with this computer. It's a shame to own the Company and not be able to get any help."

David quickly realized the man must be Mr. Luas. David was so excited to meet the top man, and eager to help, that he neglected to mention he no longer worked for the company. Besides, he did not want to get Tony in any trouble.

"What seems to be the problem, sir?" David walked into the office and stepped over behind Mr. Luas to get a look at the computer screen.

"It's running slow, it's not syncing with my new smartphone or my tablet, and I can't get it to network with the other computers. And hurry up, or I'm going to fire both you and Tony," Mr. Luas growled. "What's your name anyway?"

"My name is David, sir, David King."

Mr. Luas moved from his office chair to his black leather couch. David took the plush executive seat and worked on the problematic computer, softly singing while he worked. Less than fifteen minutes later, David had the machine running like new.

He looked over to Mr. Luas to tell him the good news, and saw that the man was fast asleep. David quietly slipped out and closed the door, making sure not to wake Mr. Luas.

"Dude! Where have you been?" Tony cried when David stepped off the elevator.

"Trying not to get you fired!"

"I knew I shouldn't have let you go up-stairs, dang!" Tony ran his hand through his hair in worry and agitation.

"Don't worry about it, I fixed every-thing," David assured him.

Tony's eyes widened, "You fixed every-thing?"

"Yeah, I talked to Mr. Luas…"

"You did WHAT?" Tony cut him off. "See, I'm dead, it's over. Thanks David, I try to look out for you and this is how you repay me?" Tony appeared as if he were on the verge of a nervous breakdown.

"If you would just let me explain," David urged.

"Go ahead, explain."

"I was helping Roger open the closet when Mr. Luas called me into his office. He said that if I didn't help him, you and I both would be fired. Guess he didn't realize I was the one his daughter told him to fire." David paused and smiled, a faraway look glazing his eyes.

"Well, what did he want you to do?"

"Huh? Oh, well long story short, he must've thought you sent me up there to help him. So, I fixed his computer, smart-phone, and tablet. He was really upset, so I just made sure everything was working perfect before I left."

"Yeah, Mr. Luas is known for having a temper. Rumor has it that he dangled a man over a balcony twenty stories high over a small dispute."

David raised eyebrows, "Dang, that's messed up," he whispered.

Tony turned to walk away, then turned back to David, "Wait a minute, who did you say you were helping with the closet?"

"Roger. Roger Coleman. I think he said he started here about two weeks ago."

"David, there's no one that works here by that name."

"I'm just telling you what he told me," David shrugged. His whole day had been strange, and he was ready to collect his check and just go home.

"No, I believe you, David." Tony shrugged too. He was just happy he wasn't getting fired today. "Oh yeah, here's your check. It took you long enough. You should have let them mail it to you. It's been sitting here for over a month. If you didn't come today, I was going to cash it myself."

"Thanks man, I really appreciate it. I've just been busy."

"No problem."

"Well, I gotta get going. I need to go cash this thing."

"Keep in touch Dave."

"Yeah dawg, you know I will. Talk to you soon," David agreed as they bumped fists goodbye.

## Chapter 16
# Old Lies, New Discoveries

On his way to the bank, David glimpsed inside the envelope. "Six hundred dollars," he mused, "not too bad."

As David imagined how he would spend his last check, he reflected on Pastor Nate's Sunday sermon, "Ephesians 6:8 — Doing good towards others will cause good things to happen in your life (paraphrased)."

David decided that he was going to hook the King family up. They were actually away for the weekend, so David decided to purchase some equipment to network all the computers in the house and upgrade them so that they would work faster and smoother.

David worked all weekend on the project. He upgraded Mr. King's laptop and iPad, installed a wireless internet connection in the house so everybody could be on the internet at the same time, networked the printers, and loaded all the latest games on the boys' computers and set them up with online gaming for their Xbox and Playstation video games. David also linked their computers to their stereo systems so they could listen to music in every room of the house.

Finally, all he had left to do was finish running the wires to the attic so that they would be out of sight. David swept a flashlight around the attic, hunting for the light switch. Shining the light across the walls, he did not see the black trunk on the floor until he tripped over it.

"Ouch," David groaned, rubbing his knee. He pushed against the trunk to slide it back in place. As he did, he noticed one of the floorboards beneath had shifted loose. He leaned in for a closer look to make sure he had not broken anything. He swept the light over the area as he reached for the loose board, and discovered a plastic bag hidden beneath.

David pulled out the bag, and sat back to take a look at the contents. He was instantly intrigued when he found documents bearing his mother's name. There were also letters from his mom addressed to Mr. King, along with a stack of hundred dollar bills tied together with a rubber band, and a book with David's name on it from his mom.

David tore open the letters and began to read. He learned that Mr. King had an on-going relationship with his mom, and it was not just a fling. She had cared for him deeply and had put her dreams of going to an Ivy League university on hold for him. She thought that they were in love, but Mr. King had a family back in California and was only in New York to finish his MBA.

David was engrossed in the letters when he was disturbed by the sound of tires crunching in the driveway. It was the Kings returning. He scrambled to quickly pack up the letters, the book, and the money, and finished running the wires into the network hub, which was installed in the attic. Afterwards, he silently slipped down the stairs to the basement, undetected by the King Family.

David's heart pounded as his emotions ran wild. He was so mad about the secrets that were hidden from him! He was mad at Mr. King for playing his mom, he was mad that there was money hidden from him (at least he suspected), and yet he was excited at the prospect of finding something left for him from his mom.

"What could be in the book?" he wondered. Wanting to give it his undivided attention and have complete privacy to do so, David typed up a quick letter to the King family letting them know what he had done with computers, games, and stereo systems while they were gone, stuck it to the refrigerator, and slipped out the door. He took the book with him to the park, found a private spot beneath a shade tree, and settled down to read.

He carefully opened the book, and was amazed to discover that it was full of letters and poems from his mother addressed to him.

David read the first letter:

"Hello Son,

If you are reading this letter, then my fight is over and yours is just beginning. I'm in a better place and I am looking down on you every day. Son, life is not always fair and it doesn't pretend to be, but have faith in God and you will win the game of life.

I want you to know that I love you so much. I know I was hard on you, very hard, but I had to be. I was preparing you for this time in your life. I am so proud of you. I am proud of who you are and who you are about to become. You are so very special — I know you think that I am saying this just because you are my son, but it's much more than that.

When I was pregnant with you, my mother kicked me out of the house, and as you know, your father had other responsibilities to take care of. Everyone was telling me to get an abortion and move on with my life. David, I am sorry to say that I thought about it. I'm so ashamed to tell you this. I had nothing — no family, no friends. I was broke, and I ended up dropping out of school. Jesse (your father), sent the money to the abortion clinic, so it was all paid for. I walked in there looking a hot mess. I had filled out the paperwork and was sitting in the examination room with the gown on when this nurse walked in. Ms. Mills was a middle-aged woman, and there was just something about her — I mean you could literally feel love all around her. She asked me my name, and I burst into tears. Here I was crying uncontrollably, and this woman hugged me, rocked me in her arms, and told me that everything was going to be okay. She said she had been waiting for me because I didn't belong in there, that I was going to have the baby. She told me it was going to be a boy, and that he was going to grow up to be a great man and God would be with him. I asked her how she knew all of that. She told me that she had seen me in a dream and I looked so sad because all of the people close to me had left me when I needed them the most. I asked her if she was a physic or something. She laughed as she explained that she was a Christian, and that God sometimes talks to her through her dreams.

I was so afraid to believe, but at that point, all I had left was hope, (sometimes that's all you need.) I found myself telling her that I was scared and had nowhere to stay, but I was going to find a shelter to stay in. To my surprise, she said that God had told her that she was supposed to take care of me until I got on my feet. At first, I told her that I would be all right, but she wouldn't hear of it. We got in this old Toyota station wagon, and we started driving. I didn't know where we were going, but I noticed we were leaving the city limits. Instead of skyscrapers, we started seeing more trees, and the next thing I knew we were pulling into this lovely estate property. I had never seen anything like that before! There was a huge house, horse stables, an indoor/ outdoor pool, pool house — you name it, they had it. I was speechless. She turned to me and said, 'Never judge a book by its cover.' She told me that God had blessed her from being homeless to being a multi-millionaire, and she owned the clinic we had just left. She let me stay in the pool house and I wanted for nothing. I know you are asking, 'what happened?'

Well, I started to go to this really nice church with Ms. Mills, and it was the first time that I really understood the Bible and that God had a purpose for my life. I gave my life to Christ in that church. I noticed that every Sunday, the pastor's son would look at me from the pulpit. He was really cute, and soon we became friends, and eventually fell in love. He actually went with me to my Lamaze classes. I had never felt love like that before, so pure and unconditional. He was going to school to become a minister. He really loved God, and me and you. He asked me to marry him. Initially I said 'yes.'

Then, one day I was in the bathroom stall at the church and I heard two ladies talking about me. They were saying that I was about to mess up Nathanial's life because I was a slut, and if he married me they would never give him a church. That Ms. Mills only took me in so she could get a write-off on her taxes, and that I and my child were mooching off the church, and the church shouldn't hire tramps, and on and on they went. I was so naive back then that I believed what they said. So I sent Nathanial a 'Dear John letter' along with the engagement ring. I moved out of Ms. Mills' house and left a note saying that I was moving to California. But I really was staying in New York. I know it was wrong to lie, but I really thought I was messing up everybody's life. It didn't dawn on me that those women wanted Nate (that's what I called him, I would even tease him and call him Pastor Nate) for themselves. I heard Nate finished up seminary in California, and Ms. Mills is still doing fine. She is the lady you met at that New Year's Eve concert.

Son, I have made a lot of mistakes in my life, and one of those mistakes was not spending enough time with you. David, you were the best thing that ever happened to me — besides making my peace with God. I want so much for you.

Well, the nurse is about to walk in. I hope the money I left for you will give you a good start.

Love forever and a day,

Mom

David was overwhelmed with emotion. He wondered about the man that loved his mother. He thought the Pastor Nate he knew went to seminary out here, but was not sure if he ever lived on the East Coast.

"No way, that's impossible," David shook his head.

"Was this the money my mom left me, and is this all of it?" he wondered. The more David thought about it, the angrier he got. Finally, he shot up and ran all the way home, planning on giving the Kings a piece of his mind. However, when he arrived, he saw a Luas Corp limo parked in front of the house.

"Oh, shoot! They must have found out about the office furniture, or that I wasn't an employee there anymore!" David stressed. He slipped in through the back door and snuck down to his room.

When he walked in, a strange voice greeted him, "Nice place you have here."

At David's alarmed expression, the man quickly continued, "Sorry, I didn't mean to startle you. My name is Sam, and I am Mr. Luas' executive advisor."

"They were throwing this stuff away anyway," David began nervously.

"What are you talking about?" Sam asked, confused.

"The office furniture, they were throwing it away anyway."

"Son, I have no idea what you are talking about. I came here to see you."

Sam continued, "I see that you play chess. Are you any good?"

"I'm okay," David responded quickly.

"Well, let's see what you've got."

David and Sam sat across from each other, ready to engage in a Chess battle. David had a confident grin on his face. Within five moves, the game was over.

"Checkmate." Sam had humiliated David in his own house.

Sam offered David some advice, "Never underestimate the power of the pawn. It may be small, but in the right hands it can be quite powerful, and can even change to a more powerful piece."

David gave a small smile, quite embarrassed by the swift beating.

"Well, back to the reason I am here. Mr. Luas has a slot open for his apprentice internship program. He wants you to be a part of it."

"What about my brothers?" David offered.

"We don't want your brothers, or anyone else for that matter. We want you."

"Well, sir, I need to make money and…"

"It's a paid internship. Trust me, you won't want for anything. Any other questions?" Sam eyed David with an expression of annoyance.

"I guess not," David answered slowly.

"When does school end for the summer break?"

"This is our last week, it ends this Friday."

"Good. Meet me at the Luas Corp lobby after school."

"Yes sir."

"Son, get ready. Your life is about to change for the better. Trust me."

"Yes sir."

After Sam left, David walked upstairs. The King family pounced on him with what seemed like a thousand questions.

David held up his hand, "Before I answer any of your questions, I need you to answer something for me. Why was this stuff hidden in the attic?" He pulled out the book and the money, looking hard at Mr. and Mrs. King. The room fell dead silent. David just shook his head and went back down to his room.

A few hours later, Mr. King came downstairs to talk to David. He came to bring some clarity to the situation and help David understand. However, the problem was he was having trouble understanding and coming to grips with his own feelings; he was a bit overwhelmed. "David, do you mind if I come talk to you for a minute?" Mr. King asked quietly.

"Hey, it's your house, Mr. King. You can do whatever you want to do," David replied sarcastically.

"David I...," he began, then shouted "What the heck happened down here?!" It was the first time he had seen the downstairs since David's renovation. The entire family came running downstairs, having heard the outburst. Everyone just stared speechlessly when they saw David's space.

Mrs. King was green with envy, but she dared not utter a word.

Finally David spoke up, "Well, you said it was my space to do whatever I wanted to do with it."

Mr. King struggled for words. He was awed; but by the expression on his face, one would have thought he had just found weapons of mass destruction in his basement. Sure, he was impressed, but also a bit concerned. However, he knew he had bigger issues to discuss with David, so he decided just to let the renovation questions go until another time.

"Okay, okay, everybody out. I need to talk with David."

The boys just stood staring, mouths agape, ignoring their father as if they never heard him.

"Let's go guys; upstairs," Mrs. King spoke up. "I know nobody is selling drugs up in my house, and if you have so much money you would think people would help with rent or something, I'm just saying."

Mr. King looked at David and held out his hand palm down and just shook his head as if to say, "Don't even take it on, just let it go." The family slowly made their way back upstairs, grumbling the entire way.

Trent spoke up, "Nice place, David." Romeo quickly smacked Trent on the back of his neck and told him to shut up.

When the door finally closed, Mr. King sighed and began, "David, I don't even know where to begin, but here goes nothing. When I met your mother, I was in New York taking some classes for my MBA. She was taking classes at the same school and she was brilliant. Not only was she smart, but so very creative, fiesty, opinionated, and absolutely gorgeous. I had been married for just over a couple of years, and Romeo was almost two years old. Mrs. King and I were not getting along at all. When she got pregnant with him, or I guess I should say when 'we' got pregnant, or whatever," Mr. King sighed again, seeming to struggle for words. "Anyway," he continued, "she was pregnant and there was a lot of pressure to 'do the right thing,' so we got married. No counseling, no nothing.

Don't get me wrong, I love my wife and my boys, but I wasn't ready for that responsibility back then and I wasn't even sure I really knew what love was. But when your mother came into my life, I found out what true love could look like, what real happiness felt like. You will never really know what a façade is until something or someone genuine shows up. Your mother was the real deal.

I didn't tell her about my family at first because I thought we were just going to be friends. But she won my heart the day I met her and I didn't even realize it. She understood me and I understood her. I trusted her and I think she trusted me. She always lived respectfully, she wouldn't allow me to call her too late at night or be in her dorm room after a certain time. We would hang out in public places or have lunch in the park. She would sing at these open mic clubs in the city and always bring the house down. She was also a part of this gospel choir at the school. I was so in love with your mother that I didn't want to come back home, and I didn't want to hurt her. I didn't know what to do. I was just going to leave after the semester and kind of disappear.

We never were inappropriate with each other, ever. Not until that last night in New York before I had to come back home. My academic program there was over. I let her know that I was leaving and that I didn't want her to wait for me. My plan was to end things with Mrs. King, but I had a son and I didn't know how not to take care of my responsibilities. The night before I left to come back to California was the greatest night of my life. Your mother asked me to meet her at the Apollo where she was performing that night. She had written a song about our love and played it on that guitar of hers. When she finished, there wasn't a dry eye in the building. She received a standing ovation and there were so many people that wanted to sign her to their record labels, but all she wanted was for me to take her to *Juniors* for some cheesecake. We talked the entire night and I took her back to campus. We tried to say our good-byes, but we couldn't. We both cried and she asked me to come inside. That was the night you were conceived.

We kept in contact by letters for a long time. I came clean and told her about Mrs. King, and she was so hurt. She told me that she was pregnant," Mr. King paused, his voice catching. A tear trickled down his cheek as he relived the moment. "I don't know if she ever fully understood how much I loved her. I was going to leave and do whatever I had to do to be with her. I really was, I just didn't know how to uh… I sent money. Anyway, David, what you found upstairs in the attic was where I had hidden that part of my life. To me, it was the best part, but a part I could never embrace.

I found out later that Romeo might not be mine and I was ready to leave, but Mrs. King was pregnant again with my child for sure, and again I felt trapped. The money you found, part of it was what she left for you, and the rest was money I had set aside for her if she ever needed anything, but she's gone now." Again, he sighed wistfully before continuing, "I wasn't hiding anything from you. I think I was hiding it from myself. Everything you found is now yours. You are the only connection I have to the life I wanted, and ironically the threat to the life I've got. For whatever it's worth, I'm sorry."

Mr. King slowly made his way upstairs, only to find Mrs. King sitting on the top step, tears streaming. Mr. King didn't utter a word. He simply walked right by her, grabbed his keys, got in his car, and headed to the marina. He needed some time alone to think.

## Chapter 17
# The Apprenticeship

David had a hard time sleeping that night. He was both excited and disturbed about the contents of the bag, was still processing all that Mr. King had shared, and now the internship — it was almost too much! The next morning, he dragged himself to school and struggled to pay attention in classes, which was unusual for David. During the second to last period of the day, David was summoned to the office. There was a package for him there from Luas Corp.

David picked up the package and took it with him to his final period, study hall, where he met up with JP. The instructions in the package stated that there would be a car waiting for him after school, and it would take him to meet Mr. Luas at the country club. The package included a wel-come letter, history of the company, CDs of their featured artists, and all sorts of Luas Corp paraphernalia.

JP whistled, "Man you are about to get paid. You are a part of the Luas Corp fam-ily now, not just a mere employee. You are going to be working with the man. You are about to get P. A. I. D.!"

"I don't know about all that," David replied, still flipping through the contents of the package.

"Dave, you've got security clearance and everything, man! You are going to the country club. That's where they wine and dine you. Man, they are even sending a limo to pick you up!"

"JP, they just said a car, they didn't say it was a limo."

"Dave, I bet you they send you a limo."

Suddenly, a debate-team sophomore stuck his head in the room, "Hey, did any of you see the limo parked out in the school lot?"

David and JP just looked at each other and smiled.

"Dave, don't forget who taught you everything you know," JP said.

"Who, my mom?"

"Man, don't forget about who introduced you to Michal."

"Uh, she introduced herself, and now she hates me because I was defending you."

"Dude, why are you bringing up old stuff? Just don't forget us little folks when you make it big."

"JP, you are like the brother I never wanted," David grinned. "I'm just playin'. You know I got your back, on the real."

When the final bell rang, David and JP walked outside. There was a stretch limo with a driver holding up a sign with David's name on it. David high-fived JP and took off for the limo. When he got inside, he took in the luxurious interior and thought about what JP had said, "You are about to get paid."

When they arrived at the country club, Sam and Mr. Luas were sitting at the VIP table waiting. Sam called David over and introduced him to Mr. Luas again. David was about to take a seat when Mr. Luas told

David he wanted him to fix the problem in the kitchen. "Yes sir," David agreed, and immediately headed to the kitchen.

When he opened the kitchen door, it was a mad house. People dressed in white were yelling, dishes were clanging, orders were backed up; it was total chaos. David cried out, "What do you need?" Someone yelled back, "Dishes!" David rolled up his sleeves and began running the dishes through the dishwasher. Within fifteen minutes, the dishes were all caught up. David then asked, "Now what?"

A middle-aged chef looked David over and asked, "Have you ever waited tables?"

"Yes."

"Good. Tables five, six, and seven are waiting."

Another chef threw David a uniform. He slipped into a closet, quickly got changed, and then grabbed the plates of food to deliver to the waiting patrons.

When Sam and Mr. Luas saw David waiting tables they looked puzzled. Sam was about to call David over, but Mr. Luas stopped him and told him to let David finish what he was doing. In just forty-five minutes, David had helped transform the kitchen chaos to order. The kitchen management  stopped him at the door and asked David how long he had worked in the restaurant industry.

"My mom used to get extra work helping caterers and hotels when they would put on banquets, and she couldn't always afford a babysitter, so she would bring me along and I would help out from time to time," David told her.

They were interrupted when one of the waiters broke in and summoned David for Mr. Luas. David went back out to the table feeling good about what he had done for the kitchen staff.

"What are you doing?" shouted Mr. Luas.

"Umm, what you told me to."

"Are you sure it was what I told you to do? Because I saw what you were doing, and it didn't even come close to what I wanted you to do."

"Well, what did you want me to do exactly?" David was confused.

"See, now that would have been a great question to ask… AN HOUR AGO! Time is money, and I have a lot of money, but not a lot of time, and if you waste my time then you are wasting my money as well. Do you understand?"

"Yes sir."

"Good. Now, the reason they were backed up in the kitchen is because our computer system is not working right. The wait staff take the orders on the SMART devices we provide, and that should let the kitchen know what to cook immediately. But for some reason, it's not working as seamless as it should. I want you to diagnose the problem and give me a solution. Listen, it doesn't matter how good and talented you are at football if you are playing baseball. Always find out what's in the mind of the person that you are producing for. You just spent an hour doing something I didn't want you to do, so as far as I am concerned we just started an hour late. Get to work!"

David nodded, "Yes, sir," meeting Mr. Luas' steady glare with an unfazed look of his own. Then he glanced at Sam who winked back at him, letting him know that everything was all right. David was irritated and annoyed, but he did not let it show. He kept his attitude in check and smiled as he excused himself.

After David left, Mr. Luas sent for the kitchen manager.

"Megan, how did David do in there?" he asked.

"He was great, sir!" Megan assured Mr. Luas. "He has a positive attitude, performs well under pressure, and needed minimal instruction. In fact, the rest of the staff's performance seemed enhanced when David stepped in to help. The kid is a natural leader, sir. Are you planning to hire him?"

"Already have."

"Wonderful!" Megan clapped her hands together.

"But not for the kitchen."

"Oh," her disappointment was obvious.

"Thank you, that will be all," Mr. Luas waved her away.

An hour later, David returned, covered in dust.

"What in the world happened to you?" asked Mr. Luas, his brow furrowed.

"Well, first of all Mr. Luas, all of your servers are in the basement and it hasn't been cleaned down there in a long time," David began. "That's part of the problem. Second, the wiring is old and your software and hardware needs to be updated. Third, there is a frequency issue. There are too many devices on the same frequency. So you are experiencing frequency interference in the restaurant. I would suggest that you move your servers upstairs, or at least have someone clean that room once a week. Also, you need to update your software and your hardware. Lastly, for the restaurant, I would have its own dedicated server just for restaurant business. And, just on a side note, it may be beneficial to mirror your mainframe for the entire corporation here just in case something happens so that you have a backup here and also access from another point. At least that's what I would do, but keep it off the grid as a security measure."

Mr. Luas shifted straighter in his seat, "I must say David, you do know your stuff. That's exactly what the head of my IT department told me earlier today. Good job. Why don't you get something to eat from the kitchen, and I will see you after school tomorrow. Tomorrow is your last day of school before summer, correct?"

"Yes sir."

Just then, Michal walked in with a group of her friends. She blew right past David without even acknowledging his presence, and stepped over to her father.

"Hi Daddy," she leaned down to hug him.

"Hey baby, how was school today?"

"It was okay. Can't wait for tomorrow. Classes end for the summer and I can concentrate on the play. You know I am the star, and this is going to be best production this county has ever seen; it just has to be! Daddy, we are on our way to the mall. Do you want me to pick you up anything?"

"No honey, I'm fine, but here is my card. You girls go and have a good time, and be safe."

"Thanks, Daddy, we will."

As they were leaving, David overheard bits of the girls' conversation:

"Who was that guy covered in dust talking to your dad?"

"I don't know," Michal answered breezily.

"He was kinda cute," another girl piped in, "in a dusty sorta way."

"Yeah, I guess, if you want to mingle with the help," giggled Michal. The rest of the girls joined in, and David could hear them all loudly laughing at his expense all the way out the door.

Later, when he got home, David was still steaming mad. He stormed right past JP, who was sitting on the front porch steps waiting for him, without saying a word.

JP jumped up and followed him inside, "Dave what's wrong? Hey, Dave!"

David broke into a rant to no one in particular, "I quit, I quit! Man, you know, you try your best and your best is never good enough! 'David, this is a great opportunity;

David you are about to get paid; David you have nothing to worry about; oh, this is an opportunity of a life time;' blah blah blah blah!"

"Yo, Dave!" JP broke in.

"What?" David snapped.

"Tell me what happened, dude."

"Oh, let's see. I just got yelled at by Mr. Luas for doing what he asked me to do, ended up getting clowned by Michal and her friends, and I have so much dust on me I look like the ghost from Christmas past."

JP cleared his throat, trying hard not to laugh.

"JP, it's not funny! I ain't going back! I promise you that."

"Dave, I ain't trying to laugh at you, but you are kinda dusty," JP grinned. "But seriously, you can't quit."

"Why not? You ain't there getting laughed at by Michal, or yelled at by Mr. Luas, or washing dishes and serving tables in a hot kitchen, or..."

SMACK! David held his stinging cheek in disbelief where JP had just slapped him.

"You're right, I'm not there," countered JP. "YOU are the chosen one. But if I had a chance to be next to Mr. Luas just for one day, I would give my right arm for that opportunity. He is the man! He is the industry! And you are standing next to him everyday. As smart as you are, you can't even see the opportunity you have.

In all of my years living here, I have never even heard of an internship where you become an apprentice for Mr. Luas. So what, you got laughed at and yelled at? Aren't you always telling me that the things we don't like to do are just a means to an end so we can do the things we want to do better and more efficiently? Learn from this dude, watch him, listen to him. This is an education that many would gladly pay thousands of dollars for, so get over yourself, swallow your pride, and try not to mess this up! I don't know about all this religious stuff, but like Pastor says, 'The flavor of God is on you.'"

"Uh, JP, that's the favor of God, not flavor."

"Whatever it is, God is hooking you up!"

"JP, you might be right, but let me tell you something."

"What's that, Dave?"

"If you ever hit me like that ever again, dude, I will knock you out!" David swung at JP playfully.

## Chapter 18
# The Boiling Point

David took JP's advice and went back to the internship with a new attitude. He went everywhere with Mr. Luas. He sat in on meetings, drove him around from the main office to the country club, and listened while Mr. Luas negotiated contracts and events. David established a great rapport with all the staff and members at the main office as well as the country club.

It had been about a month-and-a-half since David had started his internship with Mr. Luas when he arrived at the club one evening at his normal time. It seemed to be a typical day, but he could sense that something was wrong; people weren't really enjoying themselves and the atmosphere in the club was very tense. David saw Mr.

Luas sitting at his table with his head in his hands, and a half-empty bottle of Vodka on the table.

David headed into the kitchen. There he found the staff standing around with expressions of panic, and Megan huddled on the floor crying. Broken dishes were scattered across the gleaming tile, and no one was working. A couple of the employees were stooped down beside Megan, trying to comfort her.

"What happened?" David asked.

Everyone just looked at him as if they were afraid to speak.

"Well…" he continued, "come on, guys, what's going on?"

They all looked at each other hesitantly. Finally, one of the waiters spoke up "Mr. Luas just flipped out!"

"Oh wow," David breathed. "Okay, let's pull this together. Um, you two," he pointed at two of the girls, "help Megan to the lady's room so she can collect herself, and the rest of you, let's get these broken dishes cleaned up before someone gets hurt."

Guardedly, the group began to clean up the mess while Megan was escorted from the kitchen. David asked the cooks to prepare an arrangement of signature desserts in small portions and put them on trays. They were going to offer them to the diners as complimentary dessert samples.

"Let's get our game faces on and act like everything is okay, folks," David encouraged them.

Just then, one of the girls that had gone with Megan ran back in the kitchen, "We can hear Mr. Luas getting loud out there again!"

"Don't worry about it, I have a plan," David reassured her. "Come on, help get these desserts out."

After making sure the kitchen was back in swing, David stepped out into the main dining area. There, he sat down at the baby grand piano and began to play.

Almost immediately, the atmosphere seemed to transform. The soothing music calmed frazzled nerves, and soon the diners resumed conversation and laughter. The wait staff brought out the elaborate desserts, helping to set the mood at further ease.

Mr. Luas looked around, composed himself, and eventually even gave a half-smile.

Megan, still shaken but calm, watched from inside the kitchen. Mr. Luas stood up and headed that way. As he passed by David, he patted him on the back, then went in and apologized to Megan and the rest of the staff, and told them they would all be receiving an extra day's pay.

From that day on, David periodically played the piano in the main dining room; especially when Mr. Luas was experiencing one of his attacks of rage.

The members, the staff, everyone at the country club really took a liking to David, everyone that is except for Michal's boyfriend, Josh.

Josh was the son of Mr. Luas' business partner. He was arrogant, spoiled, and very rich. He was the youngest person to ever win the country club's 'Under 18' golfing tournament. He had been dating Michal for years. In David's opinion, it seemed more like a business deal than a real relationship.

One day, David spotted Michal and Josh just outside the club on their way out to the golf greens. They appeared to be in a heated discussion. Suddenly, Josh grabbed Michal's arm and pushed her against the wall. Michal was fighting back tears. When she finally broke free from Josh's grip, she ran to the bathroom and David ran outside to confront Josh.

"Hey Josh, next time you want to manhandle someone, why don't you try me?!" shouted David.

"Excuse me?" countered Josh. "I don't know what you are talking about."

"Sure you do! You like to manhandle women and make them cry to show how tough you are. So why don't you try that with someone who will grab you back!"

"Anytime any place, David," Josh sneered. "But you might want to clock out first. You are the janitor, right? Don't want to whip your tail on Mr. Luas' dime."

"I got your janitor," David gestured for Josh to make a move.

"Oh, I see, you want to be my caddy, because that is the only way you can afford to even be on the golf course."

"What? Why you arrogant son-of-a…"

"Is there a problem here?" a voice broke in.

David and Josh turned to see Sam. "Yes, there is a problem," said David. "Tell him what the problem is Josh!"

"We were just having a discussion about the club rules and we got a little loud. Sorry, Sam," smirked Josh.

"That's okay Josh. David, I need to speak with you for a minute."

"But…" began David.

"NOW!"

Sam took David into his office and motioned for him to sit down at the Chess board. At David's hesitation, Sam said forcefully, "Sit!" David sat down, and they began to play.

"David, what are you doing?" asked Sam. Why are you fighting with someone who is so insignificant? Don't you know that you are better than that?"

"But Sam, if you knew what he did."

"What did he do this time, smack Michal? Cuss her out? You don't think I know?"

"But why doesn't anyone say anything?"

"No, the question is why doesn't Michal say anything? David, Michal is my god-daughter and I love her. But she is living in a dream world. I have threatened Josh, I have beaten Josh, I have called the police, and the list goes on. But she keeps going back to him."

"Does Mr. Luas know?"

"Yep."

"He does?"

"The thing is, until Michal sees it, she is going to keep seeing him. And we would rather them be around here where we can see what's going on, versus some place else where there is no protection for her."

"Well, I got something for Josh. Where I come from, we handle guys like that."

"And what do you have to show for it?"

"What do you mean?"

"After you 'handle' a guy like Josh, what benefit do you have? Do they stop abusing women?"

"No."

"Does the woman appreciate it, or does she go back to the same abuser?"

"Umm…"

"What is the outcome, normally?"

"Well…"

"David, don't you understand you can have all of this?"

"All of what?"

"All of this," Sam made a sweeping motion with his arm. "All of what you see. This empire."

"Come on, Sam. This will always be in the Luas family."

"David, you really have no clue why I picked you. You have no idea of what you are even capable of. Your destiny is knocking, but you are afraid to open the door, and you are ready to risk it all on someone as insignificant as Josh. I know you don't understand what I am saying, but you will. Believe me, you will. By the way, checkmate." The game was over within seven moves. "And one more thing, if I find that you were fighting or you so-called 'handled' Josh, your time here is over. Are we clear?"

"Yes, sir," David sighed.

Still angry, but not knowing what to do about it, David went looking for Michal. He found her coming out the executive bathroom on the east wing.

"Michal, are you okay? "

"Huh?" she looked at David, confused.

"Are you okay? I saw wanna be Ike Turner grab you."

"Oh, he was just playing," she waived him off.

"Apparently he plays with you a lot, Michal. And I didn't realize that playing around was supposed to leave marks and make you cry."

"Whatever, David! You are just jealous that I am with someone that can handle me and is not intimidated or threatened by my status or my family, unlike you."

"What? Are you smoking crack, girl? This punk beats you and you are accusing me of being intimidated? Michal, you wouldn't know a good man if he was standing right in front of you. You must be blinded by the bling 'cause your man is only with you so he can hide the fact that he is living a double life."

"You don't know what you're talking about!"

"When was the last time he was intimate with you when nobody else was around?"

"He's just not affectionate like that. He's a gentleman, unlike you who only wants one thing, to get close to all this," Michal motioned to her figure with her hand.

"Michal listen to me, he BEATS you! I don't think that is going to get him 'The Gentleman of the Year Award.' And let's get one thing straight, if I wanted to get next to all this," David pulled her body close to his own, "I would, because you have been waiting for that ever since that day in the music room."

Michal was momentarily speechless. Finally, she found her voice.

"David, let me go. I gotta go," she whispered. She pushed free and quickly walked away.

David headed back to the main area of the country club, and saw Josh. He was apologizing to Michal while hugging up against her. When David passed by and looked back at the two of them, Josh shot David a sinister grin.

## Chapter 19
# Bathsheba

David was sick with anger watching Josh hugging up against Michal after what he had done. If only he could walk right over, punch him in the face, and then grab Michal and shake some sense into her; but Sam had made sure that could never happen. David could not decide who he was angrier at: Josh, the insecure spoiled brat who didn't know who he was, Sam for not letting him take care of matters, Mr. Luas for allowing his daughter to date an abuser, everyone else for just standing by and doing nothing, or Michal for taking it.

Furious and fuming, David thought it best to slip off by himself and cool down for a while. He snuck into the executive office area, glanced about to make sure no one was looking, then slipped out his master key and let himself into the VIP lounge strictly reserved for Mr. Luas, Sam and their 'special' guests.

David closed his eyes, took a deep, calming breath, and turned to lock the door back behind him. However, just as his hand grazed the lock, the door swung back open and in stepped a svelte, spicy Latina in a cute little black and white waitress uniform — the girl was off the chain! When David saw her, he momentarily forgot all about Josh and Michal....

"What are you doing in here Papí?" she playfully asked David.

"Uh, just chillin out. What are you doing in here?"

"I came to talk to you about your friend," she stepped closer.

"My friend? Who's that?"

"Michal."

"Michal and I are not friends."

"Well, David, you need to talk some sense into her. Josh beats her, puts her down, talks about her like a dog behind her back, *and* he is cheating on her."

"How do you know all this, and why are you telling me?"

"Because it ain't right! And, she likes you."

"She does?" David's voice brightened, but then he quickly downplayed his tone, "she does?"

"Yeah, I overheard her talking to her friends about you in the girl's bathroom," she replied, then turned to leave.

"Wait! What's your name?"

She stopped and turned back, cocking her head as she eyed David coyly, "My name is Bathsheba, but everyone calls me Sheba."

"Well, Sheba, that ship with Michal has sailed."

"Why don't you like her?"

"Because, I have taste!"

"Papí, you are crazy," Sheba laughed.

"Sheba, you are going to have to stop calling me 'Papí.'"

"Why is that?"

David leaned in close, "Because I kinda like it," he winked.

"Oh, you do?" she purred.

"Sheba, tell me why you hate Josh so much?" David stepped back, changing the subject.

"Because that idiot threatened me!"

"He did what?" David's face clouded with anger.

"He threatened me. It was the night of the dance here at the club. It was for the kids of the country club members. The place was packed out, too, and Mr. Luas had brought in all kinds of celebrity entertainment — I mean big names! Anywho, I didn't want to miss the party, but I was tired from working a double shift the night before. It was still early, so I decided I would slip out for a quick nap and come back later — it was going to be a long wild night. Well, you know how it is, I was trying to find an office that wasn't already occupied, and so I went up to the second floor to the executive wing. Well, I tried a few doors, and finally found one that was left unlocked. When I went inside, I found Josh locked in a passionate embrace with someone other than Michal."

"For real?" David was instantly in-trigued. "Who was it, Sheila, Josey, Nedra?"

"Oh no, Josh doesn't roll like that. He was kissing Romeo — Romeo King."

David almost fell over in shock, "What, are you sure? Are you positive it was Romeo King?"

"Yup. Why, you know him?"

"Know him? That's my half-brother!"

"Oh, Papí, I am so sorry. For real, I had no idea that he was your brother."

"*Half*-brother!" David nearly shouted, and then quickly recovered. "It's cool ma. So what happened?"

"I shut the door back as quick and quietly as I could, then half-ran back down to the kitchen. Of course, Josh followed me and told me that if I told anyone, he would have me fired and I would have to sell fruit on the street. Then he grabbed my arm, shoved me up against a counter, and asked me if I understood."

"What did you do?"

"I grabbed a knife from off the counter top and placed it up under his balls. I told him that if he ever grabbed me like that again, I would turn him into the woman that he already is. He let go of me."

"I'm sure he did," David chuckled. "Have you told anyone else?"

"Naw, I was going to tell my brothers, but I knew that they would beat him unmercifully and I would lose my job for sure. I need this job, it's putting me through college, well community college right now, until I can go to the school of my dreams."

"What are you going to school for?"

"Graphic design, marketing, and advertising. I want to brand Fortune 500 companies so the world will forever know their name."

"Really?" David was impressed.

"Yes, I..."

David and Sheba were interrupted by the jingling of keys at the office door. They looked at each other in panic. Both knew that if they were caught in that room, they would be fired on the spot.

"What do we do?" Sheba whispered.

"Quick, get in the closet," David whispered back, grabbing her arm and pulling her in the closet behind him, then silently closing the door.

David and Sheba squeezed together, literally hugging each other, just to fit in the tight space. Sheba started giggling under her breath.

"Shhh, Sheba, you're going to get us caught," David whispered roughly.

"Sorry Papí, I always laugh when I get nervous."

"I told you, stop calling me Papí; you might cause a brother to step to you."

"If you step to this, you'd better step correct."

"Mmmm," David thought, "this girl is feisty! And I like it! But, what about Michal? Man, forget Michal, she's got issues. Dang, Sheba smells good, I wonder what she'd do if I kissed her…"

"David, what are you thinking about?"

"Umm, nothing."

"Really? That's too bad," Sheba breathed against his ear.

"What do you mean by that?"

"Oh, nothing. Hey, I think they left. We can get outta here," Sheba broke away and pushed against the closet door.

"Wait, wait," David reached to pull her back.

"It's too late, Papí," she winked while slipping from his grasp, and hurried out of the room.

# Chapter 20
# The Studio

The next day, David could not seem to get his mind off Sheba; the girl had blown his mind! She was not perhaps in the same diva-princess league as Michal, but she had David's full attention all the same. He looked forward to getting back to the country club just for the chance to see her again. He was on his way when he received a text telling him to report to the main office at Luas Corp to pick up some supplies.

When David arrived at the office, the package was not ready, so he decided to head over to the studio wing where the legendary Luas Music Studio was housed to kill some time. The engineers were working with a new, up-and-coming artist who was trying to record a new song. It seemed that they could not get the vocal arrangement right, and everyone was showing signs of frustration. The artist was getting loud and demanding, and his writers and vocal team looked like they were at the end of their rope.

David rolled his eyes and laughed.

"What are you laughing at?" the artist spat. "You think you can do any better? And why are you in here anyway? This is a closed session."

"Your melody is all off," David told him. "The track is decent, but a little weak."

"Somebody call security."

"No," broke in Sonny, the studio manager. "Wait; let's see if this kid is an idiot or a genius."

David sauntered over into the booth, stepped up to the mic, and easily sang the melody, rearranging the vocal placement. Afterwards, he told the music artist, "You need to quit being lazy, man, and sing an octave higher." Looking at the engineer, he said, "You need to beef up that track too."

"I, uh, I don't…" the engineer began, looking confused.

"Never mind, dawg, if I had the time I would get my boy JP down here. He would absolutely murder this track for you! But I gotta go and check on this package for Mr. Luas."

The artist and Sonny chimed in unison, "Call your boy!"

David laughed and whipped out his cell to call JP.

"JP, look, I need you down here at the studio with your sound plug-ins."

"Where?"

"Luas Music Studios."

"Dave, can you hold the line for a minute? I think I have another call."

JP held his thumb against the mute button and screamed, "OMG!!! It's about to GO Down! OMG!" Releasing the mute button, he asked David, "Is Sonny there? I mean, of course he's going to be there."

"Dude! I heard you the whole time. You didn't have another call, and apparently your mute's not working or you didn't press it like you thought," David laughed.

"Whaaat?! I mean, why? Really? I mean, it's just 'cause, um…"

"Dude, pull yourself together! Seriously, this is embarrassing."

Just then, David's phone beeped, signaling a new call.

"JP, hold on, I gotta take this." After taking the call, David looked up and told everyone, "Dang! Sorry fellas, I really gotta go. The package for the country club is ready."

"Don't worry about all that," said Sonny, "we got you." He signaled for the runner.

"But I work for Mr. Luas, and if I don't handle this I could lose my internship," countered David.

"Mr. Luas is a business man, and if I make a call to him and tell him that you are working with us, he'll be fine with that. As a matter of fact, let me handle that right now."

David watched as Sonny placed the call.

"Mr. Luas! This is Sonny at the studio. I have one of your interns down here with me… what's your name kid?"

"David."

"David. He's helping us with the new record, cool? Yeah, always. Peace."

Sonny pocketed his phone and turned back to David, "Told you, kid. Mr. Luas is all about making that money. He said I could have you as long as I needed you, and as long as we were being productive. So what do you need?"

"Well, I need y'all to get that package to the country club for me, and I need someone to pick up my boy so we can get this track right."

David clicked back over on his phone to find that JP had come back to himself.

"Dude, if you ever leave me on hold that long again, it's going to be you and me, and mostly me!" JP warned.

"Whatever, just be ready. I'm sending a car for you as we speak."

"Oh, you're big time now? Sending a car for me! Well thank you Mr. Luas, Jr."

"JP, just be ready, and bring you're A-game!"

A half-hour later, JP arrived and began to work his magic. When they were finished, the track sounded so hot that everyone in the studio started dancing like they were partying the hottest Club in LA. The energy in the studio was electric. The vocal arrangements were off the chain! They all knew they had just cut a hit record.

Sonny pulled David to the side, "Where have you been hiding?"

"What do you mean?"

"Where have you been hiding? Kid, you guys have a gift that will make you kings in this industry. Why haven't you been signed or been producing for people?"

"I guess it hasn't been our time yet."

"Well it's your time now! I am going to put you guys on some work so that y'all can get out there and make some money. I ain't going to lie to you, so we ALL can make some money. Here is the thing though, as long as you are Mr. Luas' intern, you can't make any money because he owns you in a sense, which isn't necessarily a bad thing. You are going to learn a lot from being around him. I've heard about you. I didn't know your name, but I heard you had some talent, but I didn't know it was like this. So, we have to figure out how we can work this situation so you can do both — keep your internship and make some money on the side."

"Well, JP isn't working for Mr. Luas," David offered. "We can run everything through him."

"Can you trust him?" Sonny cautioned.

"JP is closer to me than any of my family. Matter of fact, he's the only family I got."

JP walked over just then.

"What kind of equipment do you guys have?" asked Sonny.

"Well, we have access to the church's keyboard, and of course, JP has some software and plugins," said David.

Sonny laughed.

"What's so funny?" David asked, not amused.

"I'm not laughing at you," Sonny patted David's shoulder reassuringly. "I'm laughing because you guys sound like me when I got started. I lived with my grandmother and she would drag me to church every time the doors were opened. She volunteered me to help around the church, cleaning up and doing whatever they needed me to do. I would have to sit and do my homework while they had choir rehearsal. I used to watch the musicians, and pick up on vocal arrangements and harmony. When I was at the church alone cleaning up, I would get on the instruments and try to replicate the choir music. Nobody knew what I was doing until one Sunday when the organist didn't show up. Everyone in choir seemed lost, so I jumped on the organ and began playing. The whole church was in a state of shock. From that time on, the church took a genuine musical interest in me. They paid for all of my lessons. The musicians took me under their wing and taught me more than I could have ever learned in a classroom, and they contributed to my first studio and my first project. It was a project that nobody heard of unless they were part of the church denomination, but it gave me the courage to pursue my dreams. So, I said all of that to say that I understand where you are and don't despise small beginnings.

"Here is what I want to do for you: first, I have some equipment that they are moving to my storage unit tomorrow. I want to bless you guys with it. Second, I want to serve as a mentor as you find your way through this industry, and third, I want to slide work your way as we partner up on projects. Make no mistake about it, you guys will earn the money you make, but I will help you get your foot in that door."

David and JP looked at each other, then back at Sonny.

"All of this sounds great," said David, "but we don't have any money for the equipment, and I'm not sure if we are ready for a major contract."

"David, you are wise beyond your years. Listen, let me put your mind at ease right now. The equipment is a gift. I wouldn't be where I am today if I didn't have people that believed in me and showed me that they believed in me by investing in me. I believe in you guys, so I am going to invest in you the same way the church invested in me. You boys remind me of myself when I was your age. There are no strings attached, but I will say this, the best way to say 'thank you' for a gift is by unwrapping it and working it for all it's worth.

"You're going to need a mentor too, some-one that can help you maneuver in this industry, and help you get through the doors and to the table of opportunity. This is going to be a working relationship, so I will put demands on you that will not only be a blessing to you financially, but will help you develop a business mindset and discipline that will keep you making money in this industry. I will help you with your business plan, accounting, time manage-ment, and the rest, and of course you will have access to my connects in the biz and artists around the world, as well as my knowledge and wisdom. All I require is that if this industry is what you want, that you bust your butts to get it. Now let's make some money!"

David was stunned speechless.

JP sniffed and stared into space, tears welling in his eyes.

"JP, are you ok?" David asked. "JP?"

Taking a deep breath, JP spoke slowly, solemnly, "Everything is going to be okay. There is a God."

"What? JP, what are you talking about?"

"Dave, everything is going to be okay because there really is a God!" JP's demeanor increased in animation as he spoke. "Remember how I told you that my dad used to beat my mom and me? Well, what I didn't tell you is that one night when I was just a little kid, my dad hit me so hard that it knocked me unconscious. When I came to, I could hear him and my mom fighting. I was locked in the closet and couldn't get out. They were arguing about money, and about me, and how if she would have gotten an abortion they wouldn't be in the predicament they were in. Then he accused her of cheating on him, saying that he didn't know if I was really his kid or not. The next thing I heard was screaming and dishes breaking. He was calling her a whore and a slut and then he said…"

JP swallowed hard, fighting back tears, then continued, "He said, 'I am going to treat you like the whore that you are!' I tried to get out of the closet, but I couldn't because it was locked from the outside. I kicked the door and shouted for him to leave her alone. Suddenly she stopped screaming, and I heard her choking out the words, 'I can't breathe, I can't breathe!' Then I heard something that sounded like fabric ripping, and all I could think to do was pray. I said, 'God, if You are real, help my mom please!" Dave, I didn't know what else to do. I remembered a scripture in Sunday school that went something like, 'Those that call on the name of the Lord shall be saved.' So, I cried for Jesus to help my mom.

"The next thing I heard was a loud thud hit the floor, and footsteps racing toward the closet. I just knew I was next. I covered my face with my hands as the lock was turning on the door, and I braced myself… then I heard a gentle voice say, "It's okay baby, Mama is here." I lowered my hands and saw my mom standing with there two swollen black eyes. She was bleeding from her mouth and she had a belt hanging around her neck, which was bruised from where it had cut into her skin, and her clothes were torn. That fool had tried to kill her that night. Luckily, he had passed out all of a sudden. My mom is amazing, she had this burst of energy, and she cleaned us both up and packed our suitcases and we got out of there.

We moved into the city into some rundown apartment that was above a drycleaner, which was owned by a family from Vietnam; they were very nice to us. My mom worked as a waitress at this diner called the Greasy Spoon."

Sonny spoke up, "I remember that place, it was across the street from my old studio."

"Exactly! Sonny, I would watch your studio from our apartment. My mom worked the night shift, and I would see people coming in and out of your studio late at night. I remember how you used to throw these crazy parties from time to time."

"Yeah, that's how we would make money back in the day for our music projects. We would have parties and sell our mixtapes. Wait a minute, did you have a little red Huffy bike that you would ride around the block, your hair was crew cut?"

"Yeah, that was me!" JP was getting excited. "I don't know if you remember, but one night I fell asleep by your studio. I used to sneak out while my mother was at work and listen to you guys producing all kinds of music. Everyone in the neighborhood was nice to me, even the prostitutes."

"JP?" David broke in, his brow lifted in question.

"They weren't that nice, Dave, they just looked out for me. Well one night, I fell asleep…"

"Yeah, I remember that night," Sonny cut him off. "Your mom was running through the streets screaming your name. She was frantic. Bones, one of my boys and bodyguard, found you on the back steps. That was the first time that I had ever seen a sensitive side to Bones at all. He picked you up and took you to your mom. I was like, 'Bones, leave that white boy alone.' But he carried you all the way up the street and actually put you in your bed. I remember your mom hugging him and telling him what a good man he was. I remember seeing Bones scratching his eye so he wouldn't cry. See, Bones' mother left him on the street corner when he was just six-years-old. So, when he saw her running up and down the street trying to find you, he just kept saying, 'So that's what a real mom looks like.'"

JP said, "Sonny, that's when I decided I wanted to do music. I would pray and ask God to bless me with the ability and the equipment to make music so I could provide a better life for my mom and my family. And it just hit me, just now, that God is real and He has been with us the entire time, protecting us and guiding us, until we would have the good sense of recognizing Him and honoring Him. Man, I am trippin' out tonight!"

"JP," said Sonny, "as you were talking, you made me realize that you are right. God has been with me, with you, all of us, even when we didn't recognize Him. And I think if we would have recognized Him earlier, well I will speak for myself, there are a lot of mistakes I could have avoided. When my grandmother used to tell me to trust God and that He had a purpose for my life, I would laugh at her. I figured she was old and didn't know what she was talking about, but I see now that she was right. I wouldn't have any of this if it wasn't for God and the prayers of those that loved me.

JP, you've got me tripping and I'm sober right now, imagine that," laughed Sonny. "Guys, I want to see you succeed. I want to see you reach your fullest potential. You have to use all these experiences that you have been through and embrace them. Use everything — the good, the bad, and the ugly — pour everything you are and everything you have been through into your music, your sound, your art, and you will soar to the top.

"You see, these are the things that will fuel your success. In life, and in your music, you have to use everything, beauty and pain. It will make you a better writer, producer, business man, and artist. Pour everything you are into what you do, and success will be your life-long companion.

"Listen, I will have the equipment delivered and installed this weekend. All I ask is that you guys do at least two records a month, and be ready to collab on some of these old projects that need some new life. We will meet twice a month for our mentoring sessions."

# Chapter 21
# The Unusual Suspects, Inc.

That weekend, Sonny's equipment arrived. David and JP decided to put the bulk of the equipment at David's house in the basement. They soundproofed all the walls and laid a parquet hardwood tile on the floor. They cut out a section of the wall to put in some studio glass so that they could see from the control room into the vocal booth/studio. When they finished, the basement looked like a state of the art recording studio, with the exception of David's personal space.

They even created a small reception area and lounge. They named the company 'The Unusual Suspects, Inc.' Sonny helped them set up everything. He connected them with a multimedia consulting firm, LeverDigital International, that handled the branding of their company, and a top line web solution called Bervee.com that gave them global exposure and distribution for their mixtapes and instrumentals. Sonny had asked them for at least two records and two tracks a month. David and JP hit the ground running. They doubled Sonny's expectation. They decided that they were going to do things right. They made sure they handled their schooling, taking summer online classes so they could be further ahead when school started back up in September, as well as their business. Sharon, JP's girlfriend, took care of the scheduling for the studio. They also brought in young engineers to handle recording sessions during the day, and at night when they were at Luas Corp. At first, Mrs. King refused to allow David to conduct his business out of her home, until David offered to pay her a substantial amount of money for her weekend shopping splurges. David figured you have to pay to play.

Things were coming together like clockwork. Their summer was jam packed with projects, performances at open mic spots, and late nights between the studios. While it was tiring, they were living their passion, so it did not feel like work; they were finally doing what they loved to do. If they were going to be the best, they knew they were going to have to put in the work. They had big dreams and were willing to do whatever it took for those dreams to become a reality.

With every project they did, their sound improved. They started producing mixtapes and sound tracks for churches and indie films. Their name was beginning to buzz in the industry, especially in the underground and international markets. David and JP's Facebook and Twitter pages were overrun with fans and followers. Their YouTube channel was getting an insane amount of hits, and David's blog was finally getting some attention. Their Bervee account began bringing in some substantial revenue as well. David and JP decided that they wanted to give back to the church, so they set their church up with LeverDigital's non-profit division called Kingdomblox.com. This took OCCC from just being one of the premier churches in the community, to becoming a household name around the world. Pastor Nate's sermons were being heard across the globe, and David's youth choir was in high demand and had become an online phenomenon. Both the choir and Pastor Nate's schedule was booked up six months in advance. People were coming from near and far to be blessed by the ministry of OCCC.

Pastor Nate had a desire to further empower the youth culture globally, and approached David and JP for some ideas. David told Pastor Nate about Kingdom Reign Ministries, and suggested the possibility of collaborating with them on orchestrating a global youth movement, "To empower and equip the kids of this generation to become the best of the best," David said. Pastor Nate liked the idea and opted to set aside funds and some real estate property the church owned in the city for a new youth development project scheduled to launch the following year. It would reach far beyond OCCC; it would be something the entire community could rally around and get involved in. They were on the move and David was excited about the potential reconnection with Kingdom Reign Ministries, Inc.

David and JP had standing meetings with Sonny every other Saturday for breakfast. They would listen to new projects, tracks, records, etc. They would discuss school, relationships, family, business, and what was up and coming for the next month or two. Sonny was teaching them the in's and out's of the business. He evolved from teacher to mentor to friend. They were all winning with this unusual union formed out of a silent desperation for genuine relationships.

One particular Saturday, in the middle of August, Sonny told David and JP that since they were heading back to school, they were about to switch gears and focus on one major project. Michal was making her debut as the leading actress in the upcoming school musical, and Mr. Luas wanted them to produce all the music for the production. David and JP looked at each other and laughed.

"What? What's so funny?" Sonny wanted to know.

David told him, "Man, with all this work we have been getting, I totally forgot about the play and the stage props crew. And to think I was plotting my way into the play to impress Michal."

"Oh, so you finally admit you are trying to impress Michal," mocked JP.

"Shut up, JP!"

"Well, I'm glad you want to be in the play because now you are," said Sonny.

"WHAT?" shouted David.

"WHAT?" echoed JP. "Oh shoot hold that thought." JP took out his cell and hit the speed dial. "Hello? Eagle One, it's Papa Bear. Code red, code red! Abort operation stage fright, repeat, abort operation stage fright! Papa bear out."

Sonny and David eyed JP in wonder, shaking their heads.

JP slapped David good-naturedly on the back, "We're good dawg. We're all good."

"So, like I was saying," continued Sonny as he rolled his eyes, "you guys are in the play, you and your singers from church. This is going to be the hottest play this county has ever seen. Luas has given me a budget, a nice size budget, to make it happen."

JP hollered, "We're getting paid, SON!"

Sonny and David glared at JP.

"What?" JP shrugged, palms up. "I'm just saying."

"Discretion, JP. But, yes, the pay will be nice," said Sonny. "So, David, what's up with you and Michal?" Sonny wanted to know.

"Nothing man, I was interested at one time."

"Was?"

"Well, yeah, but Michal and I are kinda like water and oil."

"Let me guess, you told her that she was spoiled and she went off on you."

"How did you know?"

"Because, you're not the first. But anyway, we have a lot of work to do. So finish up your projects that you are working on, and in two weeks we are going to concentrate all of our attention on the play."

"Cool."

"Oh yeah, I almost forgot," Sonny reached inside his jacket pocket. "Here are four tickets for the Luas Corp Fall Ball, which is in three weeks. These are VIP tickets, which will give you full access, so guard them with your lives. You can thank me later. Oh, and by the way, my stylist is taking you guys shopping. This is a formal event, and you boys are not going to embarrass me. Mr. Luas' son, Jonathan, is back, and they are going to announce him as the official Vice President of Luas Corp. You guys and your dates will be sitting at my table. Oh, and one more thing, I have a surprise for you boys as well." It should be a fun night.

## Chapter 22
# The Gala

It was the night of the Fall Ball big gala affair. Everyone who was anyone was there. Mr. Luas would be announcing his son Jonathan as the new Senior Vice President, and ultimately his successor to the Company. All the local employees, regional executives and offshore brass were there. There was also a star-studded cast of music artists from the record label division in attendance. It was a night of celebration and class. When David and JP walked in, they felt like they were walking into a palace.

Belly dancers greeted the guests at the entrance. Sonny had arranged for David and JP to sit with him and his entourage at one of the VIP tables. The food was amazing, the music was extraordinary, and the atmosphere was charged with excitement!

Mr. Luas took the podium at the front of the room and warmly greeted his guests and employees. He expressed his appreciation for all of their hard work and reminded them that this was a night of celebration. Mr. Luas motioned toward Jonathan and asked him to join him. Turning back to the crowd, he was beaming as he told them how proud he was of his son, and how Jonathan was going to keep the legacy alive by taking the company to the next level.

When David saw Jonathan, he was impressed with how he carried himself and the respect his presence commanded. David was captivated with Jonathan's speech; the rest of the room all but forgotten as he hung on to Jonathan's every word. He found himself quite eager to meet the young man.

After Jonathan stepped down, Pastor Nate stood to say a prayer of blessing over Jonathan and over the night's festivities. After the prayer, it was on!

The DJ announced, "Let's get this party started!" as he began to spin. Some took to the dance floor and others mingled, with everyone eventually making their way to the elaborate buffet. The tables were spread like a cruise ship, with all kinds of variations of lobster, shrimp, stuffed salmon, sushi, steak, salads, and other exotic entrees; not to mention the exquisite desserts. Mr. Luas had employed five world-renowned chefs, flown in from different countries, to display their culinary expertise. A huge ice sculpture of the Luas Corp logo was set as the center-piece on the main food table. Exotic models dressed in East Indian attire circled the room serving hors d'oeuvres and drinks.

David and JP grabbed a couple of china plates and filled them with choice delicacies, while taking it all in. The guests and many of the employees were dressed to impress. You could almost smell the money in the room.

Sonny motioned them to join him at the bar.

"What's up Sonny? This party is crazy, right?" David whistled with a knowing grin.

"Yeah… David, Mr. Luas is… known for his parties." Sonny's eyes were glued to his phone and he was clearly preoccupied.

"Sonny?"

"My bad guys; I was looking at my news updates on my phone and it seems like this Goliath Virus has just taken down two more companies — big companies! But this is a party and that's what we are here to do. JP, you okay?"

"Yeah, I'm alright," JP answered with an air of distraction. "I need to talk to you guys. I just found out that Sharon is pregnant. I am going to have to drop out of school and get a real job so that I can support her and my kid. She just got accepted into college and everything, so I told her that I would work and help her with school and the baby. Man, just when everything was going good, I…"

Sonny held up his hand, "Hold that thought JP. The reason I called you guys over here is for us to celebrate. The last four projects you guys produced have been picked up by major artists, and the singles are projected to be in the top five. Everyone has been buzzing about you guys. So, before you think what you are doing is not a real job," Sonny reached inside his suit jacket, "let me give you a very real check."

Sonny handed JP and David a sealed envelope apiece. "Before you open these, just know that this money is just for the four records you produced. There are still royalty checks on the way."

JP and David quickly glanced at each other, and then opened their envelopes. Both fell off their barstools when they saw the amount of their checks — $20,000!

Sonny started laughing, "See, JP, I wouldn't quit your day job just yet. Guys, this is just the beginning. There are a couple of magazines that want to interview you. JP, you have some meetings coming up with some prominent artists that are looking for a few of your tracks, and I hope your passport is up to date because London is calling as well as some of the islands, but we'll talk about that later."

"What?! Are you kidding me?!" JP nearly shrieked.

"Not at all. You guys have done well and I'm proud of you. Oh yeah, by the way, I have something else for you."

Sonny stood and motioned for David and JP to follow him outside. Parked out front in the hotel parking lot sat two fully loaded Chevrolet Avalanche's, one black and one midnight blue. They were sitting on twenty-two inch Dubs, and inside each one was dressed in leather and suede with three flashing LCD screens, a built in Xbox 360 and state of the art sound system. On the license plates, one read 'JP' and the other 'David K.'

David and JP lost it. They whooped, hugged each other, shouted, and almost cried with joy. JP grabbed Sonny and pressed him into a hard bear hug. Sonny looked only slightly annoyed while trying to wrestle loose.

"Wait, wait... that's not it," he struggled to speak because JP was squeezing him so hard.

JP loosened his grip, and Sonny quickly took the opportunity to escape his grasp as David asked, "What do you mean 'that's not it'?"

Sonny called to the drivers of the two trucks to back up. When they did, they revealed a matching pair of turbo charged Can-Am Spyder roadsters, with customized paint jobs sporting the logo for The Unusual Suspects, Inc. branded on the side of each bike.

"Remember when I told you guys I had someone that looked out for me?" Sonny asked them. "Now it's time for me to return the favor and help someone else. The funny thing is that I feel like you guys have been a greater help to me. I'm actually having fun again, enjoying what I'm doing. I'll be honest, before I met you guys, music had become just a paycheck, merely a way to make money. There was a time when I used to lay awake nights trying to figure out how to make the sound better. Then I got to a place where I would just do enough to get by. I was still making money, but I was making money on my reputation more than my talent.

However, since you guys have come into my life, those creative juices are flowing again! Just to see the excitement in your faces tonight makes everything worthwhile.

Make no mistake about it, you boys are deserving of these gifts, and there is more on the way. Remember, don't settle for less. Do it from your heart and the money will come. Put your all into everything you do — use the good, the bad, and the ugly to fuel you to the next level. You boys are like the little brothers I never had. I love you guys! Monday, we are going to have a special meeting to talk about future plans, and more importantly, how to handle this money you just received and get you ready for success. But right now, lets turn this party out!"

David and JP rejoined the party with a different attitude and a brand new swagger. David looked around and saw Sheba standing against the wall looking bored, and in desperate need of escape from a rich VIP's son who was obviously trying to impress her. David walked over, said 'excuse me', and stepped right in between the two. He leaned over and whispered in Sheba's ear. Her face lit up as David turned to the guy that was standing with her and said, "We'll be right back."

David easily pulled Sheba behind him onto the dance floor, gave her a sly wink, and together they broke into an impromptu Tango. Within seconds, the other dancers cleared as David and Sheba danced with a passion and fervor that seemed to heat up the room. Their eyes never left each other; their moves were of liquid precision. If they were aware of their audience, they never let on.

Michal watched David and Sheba from the second floor balcony. Josh was trying to talk to her, but Michal was too distracted by the dancing pair to hear a word he said. She wished that it were her, and not Sheba, down there dancing with him. It was not the draw of the crowd, or jealousy in the other girls' eyes that she envied. It was the passion, and the sole focus of his attention that she craved. She wanted to be the one he held in his arms, his eyes, and even his heart. That was the night Michal fell in love with David King.

When the song ended, David and Sheba stopped and scanned the crowd they had drawn, giving a quick bow to the thunderous applause. David took a small sidestep and pointed at Sheba as if to say that she was really the one that deserved the praise. When David looked up, he saw Michal staring back at him. He just smiled, then turned and took Sheba's hand and escorted her off the dance floor.

Together, they walked outside onto a balcony that afforded a wide view of the city. Sheba was breathless with excitement. David asked her, "Do you remember that night we were trapped in the closet and you asked me what was I thinking?"

"Yes, Papí."

"This is what I was thinking," David said, pulling her close and kissing her gently on the lips.

Sheba gave a small gasp of surprise before allowing herself to relax and get lost in his kiss.

Moments later, David pulled back and looked in her eyes, "I have wanted to do that since that first day."

She offered him a slow smile, and whispered, "What took you so long?"

"Do you want to get out of here?" he asked, running his fingers through her hair.

"Yo, Dave! I been looking all over for you," a voice interrupted them. "Well, hello beautiful. What's your name?"

"JP, this is Sheba," David sighed, "Sheba, this is JP."

"Hello, JP."

"Hellloooo, Miss Sheba!"

"JP, what do you want?" David asked, annoyed.

JP raised his brows flirtatiously at Sheba.

"JP! Why were you looking for me?"

"Oh yeah, Mr. Luas is looking for you."

"Okay, sure, where is he?"

"He's mingling in the main ballroom, greeting and introducing guests."

"Come with me," David told Sheba.

In the ballroom, David quickly found Mr. Luas.

———◆◆◆———

"Ah, yes David," Mr. Luas reached his arm toward David and motioned him over, "I want you to meet my son, Jonathan."

"Hello, sir," David greeted Jonathan. "It's a pleasure to meet you. Congratulations on the new position," David offered a warm smile and a handshake.

Jonathan returned the smile, "Sir? Thank you, but my name is Jonathan, and you can call me by that. Besides, it's my pleasure to meet you. I've heard a lot of good things about you. Looking forward to talking with you sometime in the near future."

Jonathan put his hand on David's shoulder, pulled him close, and playfully said, "Be careful, I think my sister has a little crush on you."

"David, can you sing something for us?" asked Mr. Luas.

"Sure, I would be honored."

David made his way to the baby grand. The lights fell dim, and the guests all turned their attention to David.

"I want to dedicate this song to the entire Luas Corp family. This is a song my mother and I wrote together a month before she died." David closed his eyes, felt the coolness of the keys beneath his fingertips, and released the music. As he sang, David could hear Sonny's voice echoing in his mind, "Use everything, the good, the bad, the ugly. Pour everything you are, and everything you have been through, into what you do."

David poured all of his emotion into the song and went for broke. He imagined himself alone with his mom, holding her hand and singing with her, looking into her eyes. His memories ran through his thoughts like a montage, all the words of advice she gave him, all the times they laughed together, all the times they struggled and barely had enough to make it. He remembered the funeral, and how dark and rainy that day was. He remembered all the times he wanted to quit, but she would never let him.

Tears sprang to his eyes, but he ignored them as he sang without missing a note. The entire room was captivated; no one dared a single whisper. When he finished, David stood and gave a quick, obligatory nod, and slid out the side door. For several moments, the room remained silent and still, before erupting into a longstanding applause. The guests were cheering and wiping tears from their eyes, David's powerful melody having moved them with dramatic emotion.

Sheba joined David on the balcony, gently closing the door behind her. She found him with his faced buried in his hands.

"David, are you okay?"

"Sheba, I can't believe I broke down like that," David groaned. "What was I thinking?"

Sheba hurried over and sat by David, wrapping her arms around his shoulders. "Listen, they love you," she reassured him, her voice calm and soothing.

David lifted his head, finally hearing the continued applause and cheers.

JP suddenly burst through the door.

"Dude! You killed them in there. You even had *me* in tears! Come on, man, everyone is waiting for you."

David and Sheba followed JP back out to the ballroom. The crowd broke into applause again. Sonny walked over and hugged David.

"I'm gonna kill you for making me cry, kid. Okay, now it's time to make your exit. Don't speak to anyone, just smile and be polite, and get out of here while I handle everything. Always leave them wanting more. Take the girls to this address," Sonny handed David a card, "and here is the key to the penthouse suite. Have a good time tonight," he winked.

David did exactly what Sonny told him. David and Sheba left the party with JP and Sharon and went to Sonny's penthouse suite. The suite was on the top floor with an ocean view, equipped with hardwood floors, a veranda that wrapped around the entire building, an infinity pool and jacuzzi, seventy-inch plasma TV with surround sound, sunken living room with fireplace, and a master bedroom with a California king bed. All of the furniture was dark chocolate, plush leather with gold trim. When they walked in, they were speechless and afraid to touch anything.

JP and Sharon cuddled up on the couch and fell asleep while watching a movie. David and Sheba decided to take a walk on the beach. They talked and laughed the entire night. They poured their hearts out to each other, their dreams, ambitions, future plans, childhood, family, career, fears, everything. Not since his mom, had David felt connected with anyone on such an intimate level. Before they realized it, the sun was coming up.

David said, "We'd better go and check on JP and Sharon."

"Papí, I'm sure they're fine. I need you to come swimming with me — right now."

"Right now?"

"Yes, right now."

"But we don't have swim..."

Before David could finish his objection, Sheba had already slipped into the water, waiting for him.

"Well..." David took a deep breath and did what any young man would do — ran as fast as he could and jumped in!

"It's freezing!" David yelped through chattering teeth.

"Not over here it's not, Papí," Sheba wiggled her finger at him. "I promise I'll keep you warm."

"Sheba?"

"Yes?"

"Are you trying to make me fall in love with you?"

"Is it working?"

"Dave!" they heard JP holler from the balcony of their room. "Come here quick!"

"Not again," groaned David. "Not now, JP!" he shouted back.

"Quick it's an emergency! I'm not playing!"

David and Sheba shot out of the water and ran as fast as they could to the penthouse suite. When they got there, they found JP standing in front of the oven with the door open.

"What, JP? What was so important?" David wanted to know.

"Dude, how do you turn this oven on? I'm starving!"

"What! Why, boy, oh you better run!" David chased JP out of the condo and down the beach.

Sharon and Sheba laughed and ran to the balcony to watch the pair race across the sand.

# Chapter 23
## Distracted

The next few weeks went by in a blur for David, and he and Sheba were completely inseparable. They did everything together, whether it was at the mall, the studio, the coffee shop, or even the grocery store; if you saw one, you saw the other, too.

Many nights Sheba came over to David's house and they played video games, sat and watched movies, talked about sports, or just laughed together until it hurt. Sheba even cooked for the entire King family one night, and served as a buffer between David and the rest of the family. Of course, Romeo lost his appetite that night when Sheba walked in, but everyone else seemed to enjoy her company. They were quickly becoming the best of friends. She was very clear with

David and never allowed things to get out of hand, nor would she stay past ten on any given night. She came from a family with very strict morals, and David respected that. When David went to her house, he met the entire family. After they all threatened to torture and kill him if he ever disrespected Sheba, they welcomed him into their family unit with open arms. David and Sheba seemed as if they were made for one another.

They were people-watching from the food court at the mall over a couple of frozen lattes one afternoon when Sheba asked David, "Can I be honest with you?"

"Yeah, of course you can."

"I don't know how to tell you this, but we need to work on your wardrobe."

"What? I look good!" David slid back in his chair and eyed her defiantly.

"Yes, you do, Papí, but you can't wear baggy jeans and t-shirts every day."

"Well, what do you have in mind?"

"Just follow me," Sheba stood up from the table and motioned for him.

Sheba pulled David from store to store throughout the mall. She had him trying on everything from business suits to designer jeans — plus accessories of course. They felt like celebrity rock stars as they took over every store they went in; their energy was insatiable.

By the time they had exhausted every hip store in the mall, David had more clothes than he knew what to do with. After Sheba had finished with him, David no longer looked like a high school kid; he looked like a young man of prestige.

David insisted on buying something nice for Sheba too, so they went back to her favorite store. Loaded down with five outfits, she disappeared into a dressing room. David looked around for a place to sit and take a load off while he waited. As he made his way to an empty chair, he dropped one of his bags. He leaned down to retrieve it, and as he was standing back up, he bumped into the back of another customer.

"Oh, excuse me Miss, sorry about that," David apologized.

"No problem," the girl replied, not even bothering to turn around. David instantly recognized the voice.

"Michal?"

"Huh?" Michal spun around, surprised to hear her name. "I'm sorry, do I know... David?"

At first, Michal had not recognized him with his new look, but as realization dawned, she stood staring at him, speechless.

"Hey," David said quietly.

Michal stared at him in silence.

"Umm, Michal?

"Papí, I need you to come zip me," Sheba called from the dressing room.

David looked at Michal and shrugged meekly with a half-smile, "Duty calls," then hurried off to help Sheba.

"Papí, do you like?" she asked while twirling around.

"Mamacita, muy Bonita!"

Michal could hear David and Sheba laughing and flirting with each other. Her hands began to shake, and she felt tears stinging her eyes. Without a word, she dropped the armful of new clothes she was holding, and ran out of the store.

When David and Sheba came out of the dressing room, David looked around expecting to see Michal, but she was nowhere to be found. He trotted out of the store and to the middle of the floor, sweeping his eyes in every direction, but still, no Michal.

Sheba walked up behind him, "What are you looking for, Papí?"

"Uh, nothing. I just I thought I saw JP, but it wasn't him. Are you going to get that outfit?"

"Yes, thank you Papí. I love it."

"And I love it on you," David turned to pull her toward him.

Just then, David's new industry standard smartphone went off. It was JP sending a text message, "Dave, get to the studio — ASAP!!!"

David grabbed a handful of one hundred dollar bills out of his wallet, handed them to Sheba, hurriedly explaining there was an emergency at the studio that he had to tend to, and that he would hook up with her later. She said she understood and kissed him goodbye.

———◆·◆———

When he got to the studio, David could hear an angry voice shouting, "What the hell am I paying you for? If you can't get the music done for this play, then maybe I should get someone else! All of you musicians are alike, thinking that the world revolves around you. Don't you know that I can make you disappear Sonny? Believe me, nobody would ever find you. Now let me hear this song you have been working on."

"Sir, it's not quite finished yet," Sonny replied carefully.

Mr. Luas snatched up a table lamp and hurled it at the wall. Sonny and JP jumped to dodge the flying pieces.

"I don't want anymore excuses! All I want to hear is some music or we are going to have a problem, am I clear?!" Mr. Luas slurred his words and staggered, obviously either drunk or high, or both.

David rushed to the piano.

"Mr. Luas, here is the song we are working on," David said quickly, and he began to play while making up lyrics and a melody on the spot.

Mr. Luas watched him, his breathing heavy and labored. Slowly, he seemed to calm, and eventually made his way over to the couch and plopped down. Moments later, he closed his eyes and passed out.

They all stared wide-eyed at Mr. Luas, wondering if he was really asleep, but none daring to check. David glanced over at Sonny and found him in the corner with one hand behind his back, holding a pearl handled .38 snubnosed revolver.

"What were you about to do?" David cried in alarm.

"Shoot this fool!" Sonny growled without hesitation.

Suddenly the door flew open and in came Jonathan, Michal, and Tony the security guard. Jonathan and Tony went over and picked Mr. Luas up off the couch.

"How long has he been out?" Jonathan wanted to know.

"About seven minutes and twenty-three seconds," JP replied nervously.

"Okay, okay," Jonathan nodded, "I would really appreciate it if you guys would keep this just between us, and I will make sure that your kindness is generously rewarded."

David stared at Michal. She looked like a frightened little girl, watching her intoxicated father being carried out of the room in the arms of Tony and her brother. When she turned to follow them, she caught David's stare. His eyes seemed to cut right through her. She dropped her head and slipped out the door, never speaking a single word.

The awkward silence was broken moments later when Sonny hit JP in the back of the head and said, "'Seven minutes and twenty-three seconds.' What was that about?"

"I don't know. I was counting while you were over there contemplating taking Mr. Luas out, Rambo."

David laughed.

"What are you laughing for?" Sonny began to interrogate him. "Where have you been? We have been calling you for hours!"

"I was shopping with Sheba."

JP started mocking him, "'I was shopping with Sheba.' Well, well, Mr. GQ, we are supposed to be partners, and while I am stuck in a cross between the Blair Witch Project and a John Woo film with Sonny about to set it off, you are out shopping with Sheba. Although, I must say you look a thousand times better."

"Yeah, you do look good, David," Sonny agreed.

"You guys act like I looked terrible before!"

"Because you did!" Sonny and JP laughed in unison, high fiving each other.

"I just gotta tell it like it is," JP shrugged.

"JP, I know you're not talking about how someone else looks, with your crazy outfits."

"Yeah, but that works for me. It's a part of my hook. I'm a crazy white boy that nobody expects to have any talent, especially in the hip hop/R&B world. I'm that silent killa they don't see comin' until it's too late. They become my puppet as they bounce to the hotness of my bait. Ooooh, I'm on fire! Dude, we gotta use that! That's a hit! That's a hit!"

"Whatever, JP."

Sonny spoke up, "David, I'm glad things are working out for you and Sheba, but we have to get this music done for this play so we can move on to some other projects. You understand?"

JP chimed, "Sheba got your nose wide open, dude. Don't let her pull you off focus man."

"Yeah, man, I'm good," David nodded at Sonny.

"We also need to record this song you just created on the fly," Sonny continued. "That was hot! David, you've got a gift man. So you ready to put in work?"

"Yeah, man, let's do this!" David was getting excited. "JP order some Chinese food, Red Bull, and coffee. It's about to be a long night."

"Finally, that's what I am talking about," JP fist pumped the air. "My boy is back! Let's get it in." Looking at Sonny, he asked, "Hey, why do you think Mr. Luas flipped out like that, and what did Mr. Luas' son mean when he said he would reward our kindness?"

Sonny smiled, "Man, I don't know JP, but you know this Goliath thing has actually hit some of Mr. Luas' partners and close friends. It actually killed their companies. Too close for comfort, you know? But the last time this happened, we all got to go on their annual summer vacation tour! I heard this year they are heading to Bermuda and the Caribbean Islands. Have you guys ever been?"

"Never," JP and David replied in unison, eyes wide.

"Well, Bermuda is one of the most beautiful islands you'll ever visit, especially in the summer time. Harbor nights, the beaches are amazing, the people are friendly, and I'll have to take you to my favorite spot — they have the best fish sandwiches on the Island. Well, I'm sure you've heard how crazy Jamaica is, and all of the Caribbean, but we can talk about that later. It's time to knock out this music. Lets do this!"

## Chapter 24
# The Unexpected

A month after the incident with Mr. Luas, the production and the music for the play was finished. David stopped by the studio and heard a girl singing the new song he had written. David paused to listen, thoroughly impressed.

"David, glad you're here. That song you wrote is incredible. It's going to be the highlight of the production," Sonny greeted him happily.

"Thanks Sonny. Hey, I can't stay long. I'm meeting Sheba for dinner tonight, but who was that singing just a minute ago? She was amazing!"

"That was Michal."

"What? Are you serious?"

"You mean you've never heard her sing before?  She is a beast!"

"Are you kidding me?  That can't be Michal. I mean…"

"Hey Sonny, how did the recording turn out?" Michal walked up, interrupting them. "Do you need me to sing it again?  I can do it twice.  I just heard it, so…?"

"No, it's fine Michal.  You know it only takes you one time."

"Sonny, why are you smiling?  If it's not right, I can do it again.  The song is absolutely beautiful, I want to do it justice."

"No, it's perfect Michal.  What do you think David?" Sonny turned to David with a sly smile.

David just stood there, speechless.

"Why are you asking him?" Michal wanted to know.

"Because he is the one that wrote the song, Michal," said Sonny.

"Oh?  Nice song," Michal was obviously intrigued, but she quickly covered her interest, "Call me Sonny. I am going back to the school and get ready for this rehearsal. Bye."

Michal turned and sauntered out of the room, her walk confident and commanding, befitting of the diva that she was.

David watched her leave, then began to say aloud to himself, "I am happy with Sheba, I am happy with Sheba, I am happy with Mi…, I mean Sheba."

"David, are you okay?" asked Sonny.

"Yeah, sure Sheba, I mean Michal, I mean… what is your name? Sonny! Yes, Sonny, I'm good," David fumbled over his words.

"Are you sure?"

"Yes, Sonny. I can't stand that girl! She thinks the world revolves around her; she makes my skin crawl."

"You know what they say, David, 'there is a thin line between love and hate.'"

"What's up fellas?" JP walked in.

"Hey JP, how was London and the east coast?" replied Sonny.

"It was unbelievable!" JP exclaimed. "Dave, we are like celebrities in the UK!

Our mixtapes are all over London. Yo, I sat in on some live sets at some underground cafes. Dude, have you checked the Bervee.com site? Our mixtape is in the top ten for downloads. Can you say 'paid'!"

Sonny interrupted, "JP! How did the studio meetings go?"

"Oh, they were cool," JP tossed the reply before turning his attention back to David. "Dave, the ladies were feeling a brotha! I got footage!" JP was waving his flip camera in the air. "But don't tell Sharon. I mean, I didn't do anything, but I could have. But I am committed, I…"

"JP!" Sonny was clearly irritated. "Are we on the project or not?"

"Sonny, Sonny, Sonny, of course we are on the project, and we also picked up two movies to score. Plus, we have ten more projects in the que that should come through the beginning of the year, all in writing and all with non-refundable deposits! Also, the east coast is poppin'. We have a couple of projects that they want us to colab on. We should know something by next week. How you like me now?"

"Very good grasshopper," Sonny smiled, "I have taught you well."

"Well, its good to have you back, and I expect full details later on," David winked.

"Well, it's good to be back. Dude, I almost forgot! Goliath is making international news. The word on the street is that this is the baddest virus anyone has ever seen. In the UK, they are singing this hacker's praises, but nobody knows who he or she is. A couple of guys in the underground are saying he has a personal vendetta against Mr. Luas and his Company Luas Corp. Dave, you better get that thing poppin' and save the family business. Your future father- in-law will love you long time!"

"Whatever, JP!" David growled, but he did not dismiss JP's words.

Sonny jumped in, "What is he talking about David?"

"Nothing Sonny, you know JP, he is always talking." David shot a look at JP as to say "Don't tell everything you know."

JP changed the subject, "Anyway, what were you guys talking about?"

"Michal, and how much I dislike her," grumbled David.

"Yeah, yeah; whatever, Dave. Yo, Sonny, did you tell him the news?"

"What news?" asked David.

"Umm, David, it seems like the main character got sick or injured or something, and he can't perform," Sonny told him slowly.

"JP?" David glared at JP with accusation.

"Dude, it wasn't me for real, I promise," JP held up his hands. "My soldiers had nothing to do with that."

"So, what does that mean Sonny?"

"Well, you are the only one that knows all the singing parts and…"

"I ain't doing it," David cut Sonny off.

"There has been a special request for you to do it."

"From whom?"

"Mr. Luas, himself."

"Stop lying! Are you kidding me?"

"Nope. You blew everyone away at the Gala, remember? Now, Mr. Luas wants to put his protege on display. Even though Mr. Luas can't sing to save his life."

"Dang! Shoot, who is the co-star?"

JP answered, pitching his voice like a little girl, "Michal, the one you can't stand!"

"You guys planned this," David stiffened, looking back and forth from Sonny to JP. "You guys set me up, I know you did. Just like you set me up with that shopping spree and used Sheba as your little pawn."

"Okay, I admit we might have facilitated the shopping spree with Sheba," Sonny agreed, "but we had nothing to do with this Michal situation. But Dave, you need to get over to the school ASAP. They are expecting you, so they will fill you in on the details."

"Does Michal know?"

"Not yet, but they are announcing it today. You'd better hurry up."

David rushed out to head over to the school. Sonny and JP watched him leave, then turned and high-fived each other knowingly.

## Chapter 25

# Locked In

When David arrived at the auditorium, he saw the director talking to Michal. She did not look happy. He watched her storm off and head backstage, and then went over to the director to discuss the game plan. Afterwards, he headed backstage to find Michal.

He did not see her in the open area, so he knocked on the dressing room door. He listened for a response, and not hearing one, he slowly opened the door and walked inside. The room seemed empty, and he almost turned to leave when he heard someone coming out of the bathroom. It was Michal, and she was only half-dressed.

"Oh, I'm sorry," David apologized quickly, politely averting his eyes. "I didn't think anyone was in here."

"Well, if you would have knocked!" snapped Michal.

"I did, but hold up. Michal, I'm sorry. Look, I know you're upset about this whole change in the production."

"You don't know what I am thinking or how I feel, so don't try to act like you know!" Michal said angrily.

"Fair enough," David nodded, "all I'm saying is that we are going to have to be around one another, so let's at least try and be civil."

"Oh, I'm civil, I am very civil. I just don't want you to mess up the production by being mediocre and not taking it seriously, or just trying to use this to get close to me. I need you to be professional about this."

"You know what Michal? Thank you," David said firmly.

"Thank you? For what?" Michal asked, voice dripping with disdain.

"For reminding me of why I can't stand you! I have a beautiful woman waiting for me right now. I ain't gotta put up with this crap from you. Every time I try to be nice, you use it as ammunition. That's fine, 'cause it's a wrap! I am done trying to be nice to you. Peace!"

David walked out slamming the door as hard as he could behind him. A few minutes later, he returned saying, "All the doors are locked."

"Yeah right, David."

"I'm not playing Michal. The auditorium doors are all locked, so unless you know another way out, we are stuck like chuck."

"Just use your cell phone to call someone."

"You don't think I already tried that Michal? I have no signal, dear," David said sarcastically.

"Well, did you try a pay phone, sweetie?" Michal returned his sarcasm.

"Umm... I would, but they are on the other side of the locked door, brainiac. Where is your phone?"

"Right here, but I don't have a signal either," she said while looking helplessly at her phone.

"That's just great, just great!" David rolled his eyes in frustration.

David went back out to the stage and sat down at the baby grand. He was playing and singing an old Donny Hathaway song when he heard Michal chime in on the chorus a few minutes later.

"What do you know about Donny?" he asked her.

"Please, I grew up on Donny Hathaway. My parents were always playing his records," Michal joined him, now fully clothed.

"Yeah, my mom would always sing me to sleep with his songs, back in the vinyl days."

"David, did you really write that song we are singing for the play?"

"Yes, I did."

"Wow! I can't even front, you are very talented."

"For real? I get a compliment from the Queen of Orange County?"

"Don't get used to it."

"Believe me, I won't. Although, I must say that you bring the song to life with your vocals."

"Okay, okay, this isn't going to become one of those scenes where we give out a bunch of compliments and then end up kissing. This ain't Hollywood."

"You're right about that, because I still don't like you. Now what?"

"Whatever!" Michal rolled her eyes and held up her hand.

"So Michal, how come I never hear about Mrs. Luas?"

"Why are you asking about my mother?" Michal stiffened, immediately going on the defensive.

"I'm sorry, I didn't mean any disrespect. I just saw the smile on your face when you talked about how your parents would have you guys listening to Donny Hathaway albums, and I realized that I've never heard anybody ever mention Mrs. Luas. But if that's off limits, I understand."

"Well, she died some time ago," Michal's demeanor softened. "It was a real hard time for us. I still don't think my dad has gotten over it."

"Is that why he has his moments?" David asked quietly.

"You mean is that why he freaks out and tries to turn into the Incredible Hulk, or a werewolf, or something? You can say it."

"Well, yeah, kinda."

"My father was actually a very calm and spiritual man until the accident. He was one of the leaders at OCCC. I guess he lost his faith in God after mom died. She was his world; she was really the one who built the Luas Corp Empire. She pushed him, and us, to always be the best of the best. I think he blames himself for her death, but it wasn't his fault."

"What happened, if you don't mind me asking?"

"No, it's cool. They went out on the town one evening. Things were really crazy at the office, money was tight, another company was trying to buy us out, and my dad was stressed. So they went out to dinner at this jazz club in the city, and on their way home they were hit by a drunk driver. My mom went through the windshield and suffered internal bleeding. My dad's arm was broken, but other than that, he was fine. She was in a coma for a week before she died. My dad was by her side every day and night, praying that she would live. She woke up just long enough to say goodbye to all of us, and tell us she loved us, and that she was going to a better place. She told my dad to forgive and not to be bitter, and then she just closed her eyes and went to sleep, forever."

A single tear rolled down Michal's cheek as she relived the experience. David gently wiped her tear with his hand, and they just looked at each other as they shared the tender moment.

Finally, David spoke up, "Thank you for trusting me with that. I know how hard it is to share those moments that nobody can really understand, and how much they mean to you. I remember hearing about an accident involving a celebrity couple when I was living in New York, right before my mom got sick. But, I never put two and two together; I am so sorry."

"That's okay, how about you?" she asked him.

"I think I relive the day my mom passed every day. Especially at night, when no one is around. My mom was my world, my best friend, my guide. The funny thing is, I didn't realize how important she was — is — to me, until after she was gone. It's all the things that I used to blow off that now make sense. I wish I would have listened more, and told her how much I loved her more. You never get that time back, you know?"

"Yeah, I wish I could get it back."

"Yeah, me too."

"So, what's up with you and Sheba?"

"Wow! What a way to change the subject," David shook his head, a little surprised. "We're cool, just taking things slow and enjoying each other."

"Yeah, that's sweet. So you're not going to miss her?"

"What do you mean?"

"While she's away at school. She leaves next week."

"Michal, what are you talking about?" David asked, not understanding.

"Oops, I thought you knew," Michal backed away a couple of steps, realizing her blunder.

"Knew what?"

"Dang, me and my big mouth! Sheba just received some scholarship to study graphic design overseas in Paris. She put in her two weeks notice a week-and-a-half ago. I thought you knew."

"Are you serious?" David asked, slightly angry and more than a little confused.

"Yes, why would I play like that?"

"No, she failed to mention it, but we were supposed to meet tonight."

"Well, maybe she was going to surprise you or something," Michal offered.

"How did you find out?

"I'm not just a cute face. I know what's going on with the family business."

"Well, to answer your question, I am happy for her, just surprised that she didn't say anything."

"I'm sure she has her reasons. Just give her a chance to be straight with you."

"Yeah, maybe you're right," David sighed. "But here is the million dollar question, what's up with you and Josh?"

"I knew that was coming. Umm, me and Josh have been together for a long time, since junior high. He was my first everything. My first love, my first kiss, my first, well, you get it. His family and my family were — are — very close. They have built businesses together. So he and I kinda grew up together and we fell in love, well you know, the puppy love thing, and then it grew. He was a very caring and sensitive kid, he confided a lot in me. Then things changed.

In the last three years, he has been under a lot of pressure from his dad. He has to be the perfect son or else. He doesn't deal with pressure too well. Something happened to him about a year-and-a-half ago. One night, he came to pick me up after his rugby practice, and he was real quiet. When I asked him what was wrong, he just broke down crying. When I tried to hug him, he shied away like I was hurting him. Right after that, he quit the team."

"Did you ever find out what happened?"

"No, he never talked about it. There were rumors, but rumors out here are a dime a dozen. I just left it alone. But he has never been the same."

"Can I ask you another question without you getting mad?"

"It depends on what you ask. No, I'm kidding," Michal laughed, "ask away."

"Why do you let him treat you the way he does? I know he has been physically hurting you."

"I don't know what to tell you. I love him, and I know the things that he has been through, and I feel or felt like if I didn't stick with him, no one else would. I don't believe in abandoning people."

"But what about your own well being?"

"I, uh…"

"Michal, you are a beautiful, talented, amazing woman with the world at your feet. You could have any man that you desire, and any man would be blessed to be a part of your world. When I look at you, I know that there is a God, because I see Him in your smile, in your laugh, in your walk when you enter a room. Even when you leave, your fragrance lingers like an echo that you were close by.

When I first met you, you rendered me speechless, but it was more than your beauty, it was your spirit. I could feel the real you the moment you entered that music room. I have thought about you and dreamed about you when I was asleep, and when I have been awake. I used to long to meet the woman of my dreams, but she is not even in the same league as you. Please feel my heart, I am not trying to run game or boost your ego, but I do want to say that if a man can't recognize the rarest of beauty, he doesn't deserve to handle that beauty, because he won't have the sense enough to protect her and value her and honor her. He will only abuse her because he doesn't have the capacity to care for precious things. Don't allow him to tarnish your beauty."

Michal stared at him speechless, another tear slipping down her face.

"Don't cry," David reached to gently wipe the tear away.

"It's just that no one has ever said anything like that to me before.  Wow..." she murmured.

Sheba broke in, "Yeah, I know how you feel.  No one has ever talked to me like that before either!"

"Sheba? How did you...?" David turned around and saw Sheba, JP and Sharon standing there watching them.

Sheba's eyes flashed with anger, Sharon looked worried, and JP was smiling from ear to ear.

"What's up, dawg?" JP laughed. Sharon quickly elbowed him in his ribs.

"Well, Sharon and JP were kind enough to help me locate you," Sheba glared at him accusingly.

"Thank God, we were locked in and couldn't get a signal and..."

Michal cut him off, "Yeah, Sheba, we were trying to get..."

Sheba threw up her hand and stormed out of the room, speaking in rapid, angry Spanish.

David took a deep breath, "Oh Lord, I've got to deal with this."  Looking at

Michal, he smiled and squeaked, "Pray for me!"

Michal returned a half smile as she said, "You can handle it." As David was leaving, she called to him, "David?"

"Yeah?"

"Thank you."

"No problem," he winked, and then quickly left the room.

In the parking lot, David found Sheba waiting in his SUV. He slid in beside her, and no sooner had he closed the door than Sheba began, "What is wrong with you David? If you want to be with someone else, you could have just told me! Are you cheating on me?"

"Of course not!"

"Then how do you explain…"

"Sheba, hold on one second," David cut her off. "If I was cheating behind your back, why would I do it on tonight of all nights? We have been planning tonight for weeks now. Why would I do that to you tonight?"

"But when I walked in and heard you talking about her beauty and…"

"Sheba, I am with you, and you are the only person I want to be with," David stroked her face gently. "I was just encouraging Michal not to allow anyone to put their hands on her in an abusive way, that she was better than that."

Sheba held up her hand, "David, you can run game on some of these other little girls around here, but you should know by now that I am grown and I don't have time for games. I believed you the first time you told me you didn't have feelings for Michal, but now I'm not buying it. I saw how you looked at her, and how you looked at me when I walked in on you guys. I'm not saying that you were lying about being stuck in the auditorium tonight, but I think you are lying, at least to yourself, about how you really feel about Michal. And until you figure that out, Papí, I can't and won't be your part-time lover."

"But Sheba, I have been honest with you, and I haven't cheated on you."

"Not yet. You haven't cheated yet. Papí, I love you and I always will, but you have to be true to your feelings and figure out what you want. I know what I want, but I need a man that is not going to be distracted by every pretty and talented face walking by. You are destined for greatness, and there will always be someone to turn your head, but you need to find that person who will turn your heart. Please take me home."

David and Sheba rode in silence until they arrived in front of her parents' house.

David cut the engine and turned to face her, "Sheba, don't go. I need you in my life."

"I know, but not right now. I love you, Papí, but I have to go for me." She kissed him quickly on the cheek then got out to go inside.

David didn't ask her about Paris. In the back of his mind, he knew that she was right. He was sad and relieved, all at the same time. The next day, without a word to David, Sheba left for Paris to pursue her education.

# Chapter 26
# A Heart to Heart

David went home after dropping Sheba off, and walked into the studio where JP was working on some tracks.

"Dang boy! What's that?" David asked, impressed.

"You like? This is that new hotness, East Coast Vibe, courtesy of my boys at Trak Fire Productions. They are blazing up the east coast. I told them all about you. They want us to come out there and do some work with them and vice versa; we definitely need to colab with them."

"Yeah, most def'!"

"So, how did things go with you and Sheba?"

"It's all good man."

"Come on, man. You're talking to your boy! You got caught red handed," JP eyed him suspiciously.

"Seriously, it's all good. We're not together for the time being, but I'm actually happy, or relieved, or something like that."

"Sounds like you're in shock. So, what's up with you and Michal? Looked like you guys were getting along."

"I don't know man. I, uh... man, let's just get through this play and get our name on the map. I will worry about Michal, and Sheba, and whoever else later. Cool?"

"Yeah, that's cool. Hey man, I need to talk to you about something," JP said, changing the subject.

"Yeah? What's up?"

"Well, you know Sharon and I are about to have this kid, and we were talking about how both of us grew up in a crazy household with crazy parents, and all the things we would do differently, you know? So, we want to make sure that our kids don't have to go through all that mess we did. We want positive people around us and our family."

"So, what are you saying JP?"

"I'm saying…" JP hesitated, "well, I'm asking if you would be my kid's godfather."

David breathed a sigh of relief. "Maaaaaan, I thought you were about to tell me that you were moving away, or was about to quit the biz or something. Of course, I'll be your child's godfather, but I ain't changing no diapers, playa'!" David gave JP a fist bump.

"That's cool, cause neither am I, playa'!" JP returned, and they both started laughing.

"So, what do I have to do?" David asked.

"Dude, just do what you do. Be there for my kid like you have been there for me. Dave, besides my mom, you are the only family I got."

"JP, can I ask you a question?"

"Yeah, what's up?"

"When are you and Sharon going to tie the knot?"

"We already did!" JP grinned.

"WHAT?" David asked in disbelief.

"Yeah, man. Actually, it was the night of the Gala, before we all met up. Sharon and I went to the justice of the peace, and the rest is history. We felt bad for the lifestyle we were living, just being reckless and irresponsible. Family is so important to us, and doing things right, and we began to realize we were repeating the mistakes of our parents. Honestly, we wished we would have waited. Fun without commitment creates chaos and pain, and a family without commitment creates a lifetime of pain, not just for you but everyone involved. How come nobody talks about that in sex education — the responsibility of the consequences, the expenses of consequences, you know? Anyway, I know I'm preaching to the choir. Life would have been so different if our parents did things the right way."

"True," agreed David. "Well, what did your parents say? Wait, wait, what did HER parents say?"

"Nobody knows, well except Pastor Nate. Nothing gets past Pastor Nate. Nothing! I don't get it."

"Really?"

"Yeah, he called me into his office and asked me what was going on with Sharon and me. I told him 'nothing,' and it was like he looked right through me and said, 'JP, you never have to lie to me.' Then he asked me how the wedding was and what my plans were for my new family."

"Wow! How did he know?"

"That's exactly what I said! And, you know, Pastor Nate is so smooth. He just patted me on the shoulder, told me to have a seat, and gave me some water. Dude! If Pastor Nate wasn't a preacher, I would think he was a psychic or something. Not like a 900-number psychic, but a for real, well, you know."

"I know JP, I know," David nodded. "So, what else did he say?"

"He said that he respected my choice to be discreet, but there would come a time that we would look back on this decision and regret it. Not regret marrying each other — he was more than excited that Sharon and I hooked up — but regret the way we did it. So, we decided that after graduation we would have a full out ceremony. He also told me that I have to step up to the plate now to become a great husband and father, better than the one I have."

"He said that?"

"He told me that he has known what was going on for years, but every time he tried to step in, it was my mom that stopped him. But, he told my dad that if he saw anymore bruises on me or my mom, that my dad wouldn't have to worry about losing his position at the church, he would have to worry about making his peace with God, because Pastor said he would take him out himself."

"Daaang!"

"Pastor Nate did tell me that in order to be a true success in career, in family, in relationships, and in life, you have to have a relationship with Jesus. That is the only way to not only have success, but to also enjoy the success you have. So, I gave my life to Christ, and that feeling you told me about when you first came to the church, I experienced the same thing. All the hate I had for my dad left. I made a decision to forgive him, not so much for his sake, but for mine. You know, I read a tweet one day that said, 'Unforgiveness is like drinking poison and expecting the other person to die.' It's the weirdest thing, I feel sad for him, but I also feel free. It's so good to be free!"

"Ain't that the truth," David offered him a high five.

"When it's time for the full wedding ceremony, you have to be my best man." JP paused before continuing, "Dave, you saved my life."

"What do you mean?"

"That day at school, when those dudes were beating you up, I was on my way to the park to put a bullet in my head because I couldn't deal with the pressures at home, and losing Sharon, and all the other mess that was going on in my life. It was like I was invisible, and only trouble and pain could see me. They became my shadow. It was like I couldn't get away from them, until you came into my life. It wasn't anything you said or did — I actually felt sorry for you. I was like, 'This poor little kid is getting his butt kicked for real!' I knew how you felt. But you just brushed it off, and somehow, I knew we were to be friends. I have watched you walk through Hell since you have been here, and everything you go through, you conquer, and you have given me the will to fight.

Now look at us, we are on the brink of something huge! And I'm not cutting anymore either. Honestly, it doesn't matter what happens from this point on. If I died tomorrow, I would be happy because I finally have peace, and it's not because of the music, or the money, or the studio, or even Sharon. It's because I have been connected back to God, and realized that all the dreams and desires I have were because He gave them to me, and He created me just the way I am, and loves me just the way I am. But, I was trying to get the things and complete the desires without Him. Dreams and desires without Him are like Disneyland with no rides or entertainment. What's the point? But with Him, you get everything! Dude we've got everything, because we have Him!"

JP's face was glowing with a peace and happiness David had never seen in his friend before. He opened his own mouth to respond, but found that he was speechless. He simply gave a slight smile and nodded, thinking to himself, "Good for you, JP. We finally found what we were looking for."

# Chapter 27
# A Night to Remember

It was Thanksgiving weekend and the night of the performance had finally arrived, and it promised to be a night full of excitement. Mr. Luas had pulled out all the stops in order to make sure this was a night to remember. There was coverage on all the main networks, a star-studded crowd in attendance, red carpet, and an after-party that everyone was already talking about.

It was going to be the night of Michal's big break, and the official unveiling of David and JP's new company. David watched as JP paced nervously back and forth.

"JP, it's going to be okay," David assured him.

"Dave, tonight is going to be the night my mom and dad see who I really am.

They are going to hear what God has blessed me with."

"JP, trust me, it's going to be great! Are they coming, or are they watching it at home?"

"I sent a car for them and bought them brand new outfits, and two VIP passes."

"Cool man. Well, this promises to be a night to remember."

"For sho'! Dude, let's get this party started!"

———◆◆———

The stage was set and the cast was in place. A hush fell over the crowd as the curtains parted to reveal an extraordinary set design. The play set into motion, and it could not have been closer to a perfect performance. From the actors taking the audience through a roller-coaster of emotions, to the dancers displaying all forms of dance from ballet to hip hop, the music married itself to the performance and painted an exquisite picture. It was a phenomenal production, each scene more spectacular than the next. David was a natural; his acting was superb. Michal was confirming the fact that she was an up and coming superstar. Their chemistry on stage was amazing. The crowd was in awe and so was Mr. Luas. Then came the much-awaited finale, David and Michal took the center stage for their duet.

JP broke into a nervous sweat, fearful and eager for them both. The crowd was mesmerized as David and Michal joined their voices in a melted harmony, singing almost as one voice. Their tone was rich and warm, the music powerful and commanding. It was the highlight of the performance.

The climax of the production was to be the duet, followed by a small kiss at the end. However, when they finished singing and their lips touched, Michal and David forgot where they were and kissed like lovers that had just been reunited after years of separation. Mr. Luas seemed a little bit uncomfortable with that kiss, as did Sheba who was watching it via internet.

The stage faded to black as the curtains closed, and the audience errupted! It was a breathtaking performance to a sold-out crowd. Michal had made her mark, and David and JP were on the map. Sonny had emerged again as a force to be reckoned with. Everyone in the cast knew that this was the launching pad for the rest of their lives.

The energy in the auditorium was electric. Mr. Luas beamed with pride for his daughter, however, Michal had proven that she wasn't just daddy's little girl anymore, but rather a woman of skill with her own voice, and what a voice it was!

Afterwards, everyone poured out of the auditorium to head over to the after-party at the country club. It was a 'Who's Who' of guests, and an extra special treat for the cast members, as they signed autographs — and received autographs from the star-studded guests that were there — experiencing a taste of the celebrity lifestyle.

JP bounced through the crowd at the country club, searching for his parents. He found Sharon, riveting with pride in her new groom. JP asked if she had seen his parents. Her face fell as she told him that they were not there. JP looked uneasy as he checked his phone for messages. There was a voicemail from his mom.

"JP, I am so proud of you," he listened to his mom's voice over the phone. "You have always been the love of my life. You gave me strength to keep going when life was dark and there seemed to be no hope." JP swallowed hard to fight the tears that threatened release. The message continued, "Tonight when I heard the sound — your sound in that production — it was like I was in Heaven listening to angels sing.

I always knew that you would be the saving grace of this family. Son, you have been the best son that any mother could ever hope for. Promise me that you will not come home, but that you will live a better life than I and your father did. Son, please don't come back. Be a better father and husband than what you have seen."

Loud banging in the background suddenly interrupted his mother's voice. Over the voicemail, JP could hear his father shouting obscenities at his mother, followed by a scream, and then silence.

"NO! NOOO!! NOOOOO!!!" cried JP.

"JP, what is it?" asked Sharon, suddenly afraid.

"My mom told me not to come home. That bastard is beating her again!" cried JP. Infused with anger, he punched a hole in the wall as tears streamed down his face.

"JP, call the police, please! Let them handle it, I'm begging you," Sharon reached for his arm.

"Sharon, that is my mother, I have to do something," JP shook her off. He grabbed her face and kissed her quickly, "I'll be back, I promise."

"JP! Please don't go!" Sharon screamed, on the verge of hysteria. "Please, please, call the police!"

"Sharon, I have to," JP ran out of the building, leaving Sharon standing there, crying and alone.

Sharon felt a sharp pain slice through her stomach. She gasped and clutched her belly as she fell to the floor, too weak to call for help. Minutes later, one of the other guests spotted her and called for an ambulance. She cried for them to find David.

David pushed through the crowd of onlookers as Sharon was being lifted into the back of the ambulance on a stretcher. She pulled him close, her nails digging into his arm, as she told him about what happened with JP and the voice message. David took off running, calling JP at the same time. There was no answer. His calls went straight to JP's voicemail. David jumped on his Can-Am Spyder, pulled the throttle back and popped the clutch. Making the bike's front wheels leave the ground and burning rubber with the back wheel, David rode as fast as he could to JP's house; breaking every traffic law on the way.

When he finally arrived, a squad of police cars and fire trucks surrounded JP's house. Neighbors were milling about, kept at a guarded distance by police officers. A broken TV lay on the lawn, along with scattered pieces of shattered glass from a broken window. David noticed JP's Can-Am Spyder roadster was in the front yard. He saw Pastor Nate talking to the police captain off to the side.

"Pastor Nate, what's going on?" David shouted as he ran over to them.

"David, I don't exactly know, but they are trying to get someone on the phone."

"Why don't you guys just storm the house, do what you do?" he confronted the captain.

"We can't. It's a hostage situation, and there is a strong smell of gas," the police captain replied.

"I have tried JP's phone, but it goes straight to voicemail," David told them.

All of a sudden, David received three video messages from JP's phone back-to-back. David opened the first one and it revealed a woman lying unconscious in a torn and bloodied formal gown, her face so badly beaten that she was unrecognizable. The video then spanned out to show the inside of the house; it looked like it had been burglarized.

The second video was of an older man, obviously drunk, and sporting a number of bruises of his own, tightly clutching a pistol. The third video opened to show JP, bloodied and beaten, giving an emotional account of what had happened. The woman lying unconscious on the floor was his mom, she was not breathing. The man was his father; he and JP had fought bitterly, and each of them was badly hurt. The gas line on the stove had been broken in the struggle, and his father had threatened to blow the place up if they tried to leave, or if anyone tried to come in. JP's father had taken his gun during the fight. The message ended.

David showed the police captain the videos, then explained how he had emptied the bullets out of JP's gun.

"Did you remember to remove the one from the chamber?" the captain asked him.

David looked puzzled at first, then horrified as realization dawned. He took off running for the house.

Pastor Nate tackled him and wrestled him to the ground. David was squirming violently and crying to be let go when it happened.

A single gunshot rang out, followed by a massive explosion.

David screamed and struggled to get to the burning house. Pastor Nate held to him fast, holding him as he screamed and cried until his voice gave out, and then continued to hold him as David cried uncontrollably, heartbroken for his friend.

## Chapter 28
# Dreams Do Come True

It was an unusually dark and rainy day as three hearses made their way down the main road in Orange County. David was having flashes of déjà vu as he rode behind in a limo in the funeral procession line. The dream that he had experienced months before kept replaying in his mind. The money, the gifts, JP and Sharon, the gunshot, JP calling for help, the three hearses, it was all so eerie, overwhelming, and confusing. David still could not believe things went down the way they had.

David and Sonny had taken care of all the funeral arrangements and set up a foundation in JP's name. Sonny had called in a few special favors for the funeral. They had white stretch Rolls Royce limos for the family and close friends, and asked those in attendance to wear white, as this was going to be a celebration of life. The church was packed beyond capacity, overflowing with people standing outside, including family, friends, the community and peers of the music industry. David's choir and band from the church handled the music along with a few special guests. Big Snipes — Christian Hip Hop artist from Bermuda, Powergirl — radio host from Bermuda, along with the boys from Trak Fire Productions, all performed special tributes for their friend.

In fact, tributes and condolences poured in from around the country and the world. It was the first funeral that David had ever seen with three caskets. Pastor Nate preached the eulogy magnificently, delivering a powerful message that honored the lives of the deceased, but also brought responsibility and reality to the forefront of those attending. He talked about the two most important days in a person's life, today and 'that day.'

"'That day' is the day when you give account to God for all that you have done in your life — the good, the bad, and the ugly," preached Pastor Nate. "That day is when eternity truly begins, but you can't wait to determine what your eternity will be on 'that day.' No friends, that has to be decided today."

Pastor Nate went on to say that it is at moments like this that we stop and think about the big picture, and realize that we are not immortal. Whether we like it or not, we will have to face our creator. When we do, our creator will ask us if we received His free gift in the person of Jesus Christ, and did we finish the assignment that He gave to us on Earth, or if we simply did our own thing. We will have to give an answer.

The pastor's words had a sobering effect, but they were wrapped in love and heart-felt compassion. The church was silent as the pastor continued.

Pastor Nate addressed those who once believed in God, but somewhere along the way got sidetracked and lost focus, or 'got busy.' He told them that God has been with them all along, still loving them, and blessing them, and protecting them. He reminded the congregation that God was not angry with them, but desired the very best for them, and was simply waiting for them to come back home. Much like the prodigal son, they may have left their place in the palace trying to make a name for themselves, perhaps having lost everything along the way. But it was time to come back home.

"God is waiting, longing for your return." Pastor Nate wiped at a slow tear that slipped from his eye as he continued, "Many of you have the fortune and fame, the money and the toys, but deep down, you have lost your joy. Your peace is gone, and there is a hole on the inside that hasn't been filled. If we could measure that hole, it would be the size of God Himself, because He is the only one that can fill it."

Pastor Nate reminded everyone of what Jesus did on the cross just to become our friend. How He continues to fight for us and protect us, and continues to draw us with His love, even when we are not thinking about Him. He asked those that wanted to come home and commit their lives to doing things God's way to lift their hands. Hundreds of hands went up as tears came streaming down. He finished by saying, "Even in tragedy, JP's life is still speaking today and is producing more life. It doesn't matter how you start as much as how you finish. JP finished well!

---

As they pulled up to the graveside where the caskets were to be laid, David reflected over Pastor Nate's message. There had not been a dry eye in the church that morning. The love and presence of God was like a blanket; if not for the haunting presence of the three caskets, it would have been almost easy to forget that it was a funeral.

David had tried to hold strong for Sharon's sake, and he did, until they played the video. The video was a portfolio of highlights of JP's life. At the end was a surprise message from JP that he had recorded earlier in the day before the play. In it, he expressed his love to Sharon and their unborn son, to Pastor Nate, all his friends and colleagues, and last but not least, to David.

He made David promise to finish what they had started. It was like JP had somehow known it was the end for him, but he was at peace.

After the funeral, there was a catered reception at the country club. Many of JP's friends found David to pay their respects and let him know that if he needed anything, to never hesitate to call. Leon, the one who had built the laptop for David, told him that if there was anything he could be a part of or help with, to please let him know. Several commented on the change they had seen in JP, and told David about how JP had told them all about him. They all simply wanted the opportunity to honor JP by being a help to David and the company the two of them had built. David realized then that even though his friend was gone, a new era was just beginning.

# Chapter 29
# The Marina

Three months passed since JP died. Sharon had given birth to their son, naming him Absalom after her grandfather. She was still running the home studio and generating a good income, and David was still receiving royalty checks from the projects he and JP had worked on together. However, David had withdrawn. He stopped writing and singing songs, stepped down from the internship position with Mr. Luas, and stopped producing for Sonny. David continued to attend church, but just as a spectator. The choir was full of capable musicians. David would come late to hear the sermon and leave early so he would not have to talk to anyone. He simply faded into the background, immersed in his grief.

Mr. King saw David moping around day after day; it was almost as if his life had been taken from him too. Three months were long enough, he could not stand idly by and watch his son waste away; the boy had too much potential, and he had come too far.

"Come on David, let's go out to the marina," he said to David one Saturday afternoon in February. When David hesitated, he continued, "Come on now, the sun is out and it's too nice a day to stay cooped up inside. Besides, I've got something I want to show you."

David grudgingly agreed, and rode with Mr. King out to the marina. When they arrived, he followed him to a beat-up, run down old boat.

"Well, here she is!" Mr. King smiled proudly at the boat.

"Here who is?" David asked, confused.

"My baby! She has saved my life a number of times."

"You mean she held up in bad weather?"

"You could say that," Mr. King chuckled.

"Oh yeah? How many times have you taken her out?"

"None."

"None?" Now David was really confused. "I don't get it."

Mr. King laughed and said, "You will. Let me explain. When I found this boat, I thought it would be a great family project for me and the boys, something to work on together, to strengthen our bond, you know? However, when the boys saw what kind of shape she was in, they just laughed, like spending time together was a prison sentence or something. You know, I lost my dad and mom at an early age. Man, I wish I would have listened to them more," Mr. King said wistfully. "Anyway, since then, I've used her as my own personal little getaway. Whenever I want to get away from Mrs. King," he winked at David playfully, "or just slip away to relax, I come here. No one ever bothers me here, well, outside of a few hecklers."

"Hecklers?" David asked.

"Yeah, some of the 'neighbors,'" he motioned to the other boats, nice, large, fancy yachts docked all across the marina. "They only let me keep her here because I handle the accounts for the marina, as well as most of its board members and other influential boat owners that dock here, at my firm. So, they gave me a pass, but I still hear static most times I come here from the other boat owners wanting me to fix up my girl."

"I see," said David.

"Not yet, but you will," replied Mr. King. "Sit down, let's talk."

David and Mr. King sat down on the dock, feet dangling over the water. Mr. King took a deep breath, and stared out across the ocean, his expression one of a wise man about to unfold the mysteries of life. David was all ears.

"There are all sorts of storms in life, David. Hurricanes, tornadoes, typhoons, but the biggest storms we face are not external, but internal, on the inside. They're the things no one else can see directly, but we feel them just the same. Often times, they're slow moving storms, leaving behind a lot of damage. We learn how to wear masks, hide our emotions, to keep from causing others discomfort. Yet, behind our masks, we're angry, sad, lonely, depressed, misunderstood, discouraged, confused — a whirlwind of emotions. Still, we try to smile and pretend everything is okay. Those slow moving storms, they like to linger until they take us down, or we take them down, or at least learn how to manage them. Do you understand what I'm saying?"

"Kind of." David focused his gaze on the water, his expression indicative of deep, intense thought.

"This boat has become my place of refuge, where I come to reflect and deal with the storms in my life. It's kind of like Superman's 'Fortress of Solitude.' Here, I don't have to be a dad, boss, or husband, I can just be Jesse. All my issues and my flaws, I don't have to hide them here, I can be who I am and get the help I need."

"What do you do here?"

"Sometimes I just think, or read, or listen to the water, or music, whatever. But mostly, I find myself praying and listening to the voice of God, listening for direction and instruction. He will never fail you, David. If you can just get quiet enough to listen. Sometimes, our emotions and egos are so loud that they drown out the voice of God. However, if you quiet yourself, tune your ear to the voice of God, and obey, you will have solid success in your life. I know I haven't been much of a father to you, but this is as fatherly as it gets. These are keys to life. Son, I have seen your spirit crushed twice; first when your mom passed and now having lost your best friend, JP. I see the storms forming in your life and preparing to take up residence inside you. But you are stronger than this, and your destiny is far bigger than this."

"But…" David began to object.

"Mr. King held up his hand, "No, let me finish. Neither your mother nor your friend would want you to stop your progress. They would tell you to keep fighting and embrace everything God has for you. But you have to deal with these storms. I can't do it for you. You have to do it for yourself. So I am giving you access to my Fortress of Solitude, to get away and deal with whatever you need to deal with. But the key is drawing closer to God. I want to give you this journal too, to write your thoughts in, and your prayers, and whatever else comes to mind."

Mr. King opened the brown paper bag he had been carrying and pulled out a brown, leather-bound journal with a locking mechanism and an old Mont Blanc pen. David could tell that the journal and the pen were both of great value, but for David the value was not monetary, it was the connection that he was making with his father that was priceless.

"Man, I didn't expect all of this today," David held the journal and pen as if they were fragile treasures. "Thank you so much," his voice caught with emotion. He paused, cleared his throat and grinned, "So, if this boat is supposed to be the 'Fortress of Solitude' and has saved your life, don't you think we should save her life and give her a makeover or something? I'm just saying."

Mr. King smiled and pulled David into a playful, loose headlock as they looked at the boat.

"Yeah," nodded Mr. King, his eyes taking on a faraway, thoughtful look. "We could do something like that. Oh yeah, before I forget, I have something else for you."

Mr. King stepped onto the boat and disappeared below, then resurfaced with a red acoustic guitar. "This was your mother's. She and I would go to Central Park and eat hotdogs from the street vendors, and she would sing to me and play this guitar. David, it's crazy but I see so much of her in you."

David just looked away, staring out across the water.

"Okay David, I know, but I am going to leave it here for you. It's yours, whenever you're ready."

While David did not have the words to express the wide range of emotions he was feeling, he was grateful.

———◆———

Over the course of the next four months, David spent day and night working on renovating the boat. David was able to complete his high school requirements for graduation via online courses, which enabled him to focus most of his effort on the boating project. He studied up online and asked questions of the other boat owners, learning all he could about boating.

He made a few new friends there that were eager to help. It became the talk of the marina, Jesse King was finally fixing up that old eyesore he called a boat. Several nights, David did not even bother to go home. He just stayed on the boat and wrote in his journal. It became his therapy. The days melted into weeks, and the weeks into months. The boat quickly became David's second home; some would even argue that it was his home.

Every day, David made more progress on the boat, but more importantly, he made progress within himself. In his writings, he found himself inspired with new songs, and even a few movie ideas; his passion was coming back. He soon found that he felt like himself again.

David upgraded the interior of the boat with plush new carpet and brand new, modern furniture for the office and lounge area that suited his personality and taste. It included a small, state of the art music/video studio and screening room with a docking station for his laptop, and a full surround sound setup with subwoofer. It was like having a movie theatre on the water.

Mr. King was so excited that someone in the family was finally taking an interest in the boat project that he set aside a sizable sum of money to help with the renovations. The boat was large enough to comfortably sleep the entire King family, including David. However, Mr. King, still stung by the rest of the family for shooting him and the project down in the beginning, decided to turn the four-cabin boat into a two-cabin master suite with a luxury entertainment area.

Mr. King acted like a big kid with a shiny new toy, adding more luxury items to the boat and going way over budget. He sprung for a barbeque grill and a landing that could hold two jet skis. Their excitement was contagious; almost daily, their marina neighbors were dropping by and offering suggestions and contacts to their connections in the boating world. When the project was finished, the boat had transformed from an old, rundown, eyesore on water to an impressive, glamorous mini-yacht.

# Chapter 30
# Destiny Calls

One sunny afternoon in May, while David was working on the boat at the marina as usual, he received a call from Mr. King asking a favor. Mr. King was pressed for time on his way to a meeting and the King boys had forgotten their lunch that day. Mr. King asked David if he would pick something up for them and drop it off at Luas Corp. All three, Romeo, Derrick and Trent were interning for the summer there, per David's recommendation.

"No problem, I'll take care of it," agreed David.

It had been a while since David had been to the Luas Corp headquarters, and he found that he was looking forward to seeing his old friends there. He hurried and got cleaned up, then grabbed his laptop to take with him so he could show Sonny the before and after pictures of the boat, and go over some new project ideas.

When David arrived, he felt like he walked into a sea of lost sheep. Interns milled about trying to find their way, get registered, and be on time all at the same time. David finally located his brothers, along with Mrs. King, who was arguing with an obviously flustered well-dressed older lady at the registration table.

David lightly slapped Romeo on his shoulder, "Hey cupcake."

Romeo spun around, smiling with expectation, until he saw that it was David.

"What's the matter? You were hoping for someone else? Sorry to disappoint you," David told him.

"Why are you even here?" Romeo scowled. "Didn't you get fired?"

"Don't get mad at me because you have to get dressed up all summer while I'm just chilling."

"Oh, that's right; you're working with my dad fixing up that old tugboat. Hey guys," Romeo called to his brothers, "look, it's Jack Sparrow!"

"Hey Jack," Derrick and Trent shouted in unison, commanding the attention of the crowd.

Romeo glared at David, "I don't care how much you suck up to *my* father, you will never be a true son, or a part of this family. You are just a player's mistake, you bast... oof!"

Before Romeo could finish, David grabbed him in a bear hug and squeezed with all his might. Romeo could barely breathe, let alone speak.

David whispered in his ear, "I told you before, you had one more time to disrespect me or my mother, and you have done both. I am more of a son than you ever will be. I know your secret, Romeo, or is it Juliet? Wouldn't your father like to know that not only does he have three sons, but a daughter too? Look, I don't know why, and I'm not here to judge, but here's a word of advice: don't piss off the guy that's feeding you and knows what you've been hiding. Enjoy your lunch."

David dropped the bag of food on the floor and walked away. Romeo clutched his sides and gasped for air while his brothers looked worried, asking if he was all right.

David sauntered through the foyer of Luas Corp like he owned the place. As he made his way to the elevator, a young man hurriedly brushed by him. David recognized him as his replacement in maintenance from a little over a year ago.

David wondered to himself, "Now, what was his name? Robert? No, Roy, umm, oh yeah, Roger! Roger Coleman."

David called after him, "Roger! Hey, Roger Coleman, right?" The young man kept on walking as if he never even heard David. "Huh, strange," David muttered, and then shrugged it off as he got on the elevator.

When David got off the elevator on the next floor, he found Sonny standing there talking with a few of the studio engineers along with Tony, the head of security, and Mr. Luas' son, Jonathan. Their conversation halted immediately when they saw

David. No one from Luas Corp had seen him since the funeral.

"Well it's about time," Sonny said softly in wonder.

David smiled and they all rushed him, hugging him, and shaking his hand, laughing and talking all over each other. All except for Jonathan, who quietly stood back and watched the scene unfold.

"Come on, guys, it hasn't been that long," David laughed.

"Man, it's just so good to see you," Sonny told him.

"Yeah, it's good to be seen. I've missed you guys, believe it or not."

"How have you been?"

"I'm good, weathering the storm. I was lost for a minute after JP, but I'm finding my way and I know things are going to be alright."

"I feel you man. It's not easy, I know, but what does the song say? 'I once was lost but now I'm found.' I'm glad your back. I'm sure we'll catch up soon."

"Yeah, definitely. I have some stuff to show you that I know you'll like."

Sonny smiled. He knew that whatever David had going on, it was going to be good, and it was going to prosper.

Jonathan finally broke in, "Sonny, don't forget about your presentation today for the summer students during the orientation. I will talk to you guys later. David, it's good seeing you again, hope you come around more often." Jonathan patted David on the shoulder as he made his exit and disappeared around the corner.

Tony spoke up, "David before you get too comfortable and disappear with Sonny, run me over to Chick-fil-A so I can grab something to eat, if you will. My ride is in the shop, and I only have an hour before I have to be back."

"Sure, Tony, I probably owe you anyway. Sonny, I will be right back."

"Cool Dave," Sonny nodded, "looking forward to it, and bring me back something while you're at it."

"Geez, a brother comes back to visit and you put him to work right away," David teased.

David and Tony made their way to the parking lot, and climbed in David's Chevy Avalanche.

David asked him, "Yo, how is my replacement working out?"

Tony looked confused, "What are you talking about?"

"You know, the cleaning guy, Roger Coleman."

Tony looked confused for a moment, "David, I remember you asked me about him before, but nobody by that name works at Luas Corp."

"Hmm, that's strange," David mused.

They arrived at the restaurant, went inside and ordered, then settled down at a booth and began catching up before David brought it back up again.

"Tony, I saw Roger Coleman leaving Luas Corp as I was coming up to see you guys. He seemed pretty focused. He didn't speak, almost knocked me over when he walked by, and didn't even turn around when I called his name. The poor guy, you all must be working him too hard."

Tony laughed, "Maybe, but you must not have this dude's name right, because I'm telling you that nobody by that name works at Luas Corp."

David opened his mouth to respond, but was immediately distracted by a breaking news announcement coming over the restaurant's big screen TV.

"Breaking news, Goliath holds Luas Corp hostage! What started out as a summer employment orientation has turned into a nightmare as hundreds of students are being held hostage by what seems to be a computer virus called 'Goliath.' A video message was broadcast during Mr. Luas' opening remarks to the new summer workers. This same video message was sent to our OCC News studio as well. The message claims that unless Luas Corp wires one billion dollars to a specified off shore account, the virus will be released. If that happens, it will destroy valuable company information, resulting in the complete demise of Luas Corp itself, not to mention the company's thousands of global employees that would suddenly be out of work. Goliath has also warned that no one is to leave the building. Any attempts to do so will be detected by booby-traps set throughout the building, and the company's computers will simultaneously explode with the threat of fatal results. The virus is said to be released in just two hours."

# Chapter 31
# Taking on the Giant

David and Tony's eyes were glued to the screen, as were those of the entire restaurant, patrons and employees. The place fell silent in shock, save for the reporter on the TV. Tony took off out the door, shouting into his walkie-talkie, but getting no response. David followed quickly behind.

"Get me back there now!" Tony yelled to him as they jumped in David's truck.

David squealed tires out of the parking lot while Tony kept dialing and trying to radio in. "I can't reach anyone!" "What about Mr. Luas' private cell?"

"We are only allowed to call that number in extreme emergencies," replied Tony.

"Tony, I think this qualifies."

As they pulled back into the parking lot of Luas Corp, Tony had to flash his head of security badge to get past the police guards. Emergency vehicles circled the outside of the building, and police helicopters swirled overhead. S.W.A.T. teams had already arrived, and snipers were strategically set in place.

"Tony, what's that number?" David asked again. "I'll see if I can get Mr. Luas while you deal with this."

David snatched up his cell phone and, with trembling fingers, frantically pounded the key pad, "Hello...hello...Mr. Luas?!"

A gruff and panicked voice squawked through the receiver, "Who is this? You'll never get away with this! You no good, son of a...."

"Mr. Luas, it's me, David!"

"David?" Mr. Luas shot back, his confusion obvious.

"David King, sir."

"Oh. I'm sorry son. For a minute there, I thought you might be the hacker. This idiot is trying to extort a billion dollars from me!"

"I know. I saw the news, sir. But I can stop him."

"How? They have all the computers here at the office wired to explode if we so much as touch them, and they have already fried all the computers on the first floor. None of my IT guys know what to do. Besides that, nobody can leave! If anyone even tries…"

"What was that?" David nearly dropped the phone as the deafening noise shot through the receiver. "Mr. Luas, are you okay? Are you still there, are you all right? Mr. Luas? Hello?"

"I'm here. All the computers just went on the second floor."

"Sir, listen to me. I can stop this guy. But I am going to need access to your personal code and password for the mainframe, and your private entrance at the club. Do you remember my first day working for you?"

"David, you are either brilliant or you are about to kill my company and send this town into an epic recession. Either way, we are depending on you, son. Here is my code…"

David closed his eyes to memorize the info, and suddenly it felt as if the world was moving in slow motion although his mind was racing.

Thinking aloud, David mused, "Who would have ever imagined when I started with this company just under a year-and-a-half ago that I would be here, with the fate of the city, and the livelihood of people worldwide, resting on my shoulders. Wow, things have certainly changed."

"David, are you still there?" Mr. Luas cried over the phone.

"Yes sir!"

"Is anyone with you?"

Tony, who was standing close by listening, heard Mr. Luas' question and shook his head at David, mouthing, "Don't tell him I'm here."

David hesitated, "Umm," he could not force the lie, "yes, Tony is with me."

Tony glared at David, shaking an angry fist. David just shrugged.

"Great! That's good," declared Mr. Luas.

David and Tony exchanged looks of disbelief, confused as to why Mr. Luas would be glad Tony was with David and not inside.

"Tell Tony to take you through the tunnels to my personal emergency entrance," continued Mr. Luas, "and you can use my computer — they say it's the fastest thing out — to link to the mainframe."

"Thanks Mr. Luas, but I think I'd better use what I have. I'm familiar with how it works, it's been tried and tested, and we only have one shot at this thing."

"What kind of computer do you have?"

"Mr. Luas, it's better that you don't know. Just trust me."

David simply could not bring himself to tell Mr. Luas that the computer was a 'Leon' built by an ex-convict, at least not until they got the victory.

"Fine David, but hurry up, we only have forty-five minutes left," Mr. Luas barked. "Not only will this affect the city, but all of our global partners as well. So do good, son. And David, if you pull this off, you will be set for life — you and your family."

"Ok, Mr. Luas, I will talk to you in forty-five minutes. Oh, and Mr. Luas, have security check the supply closet by your office, I have a feeling you may find some evidence there."

David hung up the phone and headed out to the country club with Tony. Tony led David through the tunnels.

"Is Mr. Luas Batman or something?" joked David.

"David, you have no clue who Mr. Luas really is," Tony said seriously. "He is a mogul yes, but there is a dark side to him, especially since his wife died."

"They were hit by a drunk driver, right?"

"That's what he wanted everyone to believe, even his family. But that's not what actually happened. There was a hit put out on Mr. Luas and there was an actual war going on."

"You mean like some kind of mob or mafia thing? Come on Tony, that's just movie stuff, right?"

"David, I was here, I saw the bodies. Mr. Luas has hurt a lot of people, and a lot of innocent bystanders have been casualties of war in the process. David, hear me, when it's your time to rule, do it with compassion and with the fear of God. Because the seeds we sow always comeback bigger and harder, to the degree that it doesn't just affect us, but everyone connected to us. You have a great heart. Stay pure and true, and you will have great success. If you stray, be quick to get it right."

Tony stopped to turn and look David directly in the eye. He repeated, "If you stray, be quick to get it right, first with God, then yourself, and whoever you did wrong, because it *will* come back."

Tony turned back and opened a door that blended with the wall so well, it was almost undetectable. "Here we are man, do your thing," he motioned to David.

They slipped inside the large room of computers, and David quickly connected his laptop to the server and hacked into the mainframe. "Man, it's a good thing that Mr. Luas listened to my recommendation and kept this access point to the mainframe off grid so that this location would remain undisclosed. I guess it pays to listen to a former hacker. Here Tony, take my phone and update me on what Mr. Luas is saying." David handed Tony his phone so he could read off the text messages as they came in from Mr. Luas.

"They just lost all the computer workstations on the fourth floor," Tony told him.

David's fingers flew across the keys of the Leon. He found the source of the virus and where it was embedded in the mainframe. A webcam video display popped up on David's laptop screen. It was the same young man that he saw earlier that day, the same one that he had helped with the locked door at Luas Corp over a year ago.

"So I guess it's safe to say that your name is not Roger?" David asked bluntly.

"Nope! I can't believe they sent a former janitor to try and stop me," the hacker laughed. "I am about to destroy Luas Corp, and its subsidiaries, globally!"

While the hacker was talking, David continued to work. Tony kept David updated on the texts still coming in, "They found the closet, and it's full of enough explosives to level the building."

David never flinched; he just kept working without stopping. He began talking to himself, "I can't find the remote trigger frequency to stop the virus and keep the bombs from going off."

"What are you going to do David King?" the hacker mocked him from the computer screen. "You can't stop the virus *and* the explosions. So, do you save the money or the people?"

"Lord, help me!" David prayed aloud.

"God can't help you on this one," the hacker scoffed.

All the lights in the room flickered.

"Five minutes!" Tony shouted.

"That's it!" David exclaimed, his expression registering fresh revelation. With a few swift keystrokes, David uploaded Slingshot to the mainframe. Slingshot subsequently protected all of its data and backed it up to three different locations, which juggled the info in a manner that no one could get a lock on it. Next, David killed the power to the Luas Corp building and implemented a jamming signal into the mainframe server, which bought him more time.

He smiled at the screen and whispered, "Watch this." David tapped into Slingshot's most powerful feature, the 'stone throw.' It severed the virus from its host and sent it back to its origin. All the while, it set a tracer on the hacker and relayed his whereabouts and picture to the local authorities and FBI. It also locked onto the hacker's computer and its networks, and stripped its contents to a backup location for evidence purposes.

David sat back and smiled at the perplexed hacker's image on his computer screen, "They're coming for you."

It was over. Slingshot had worked. For David, the victory was bittersweet. All he could think of was JP. "I sure wish you could have been here," he whispered to JP's memory.

Sighing, David pushed back in his chair and spun around to find a pearl handled snub nose .38 caliber gun mere inches from his face.

"Tony, what are you doing?"

"Sorry David, you weren't supposed to beat this thing."

"So that's how he knew my name. I guess Michal was telling me the truth after all, she didn't get me fired, *you* did. What the heck are you doing? Why, Tony?"

"David, I tried to protect you from all of this! You have no clue of what's going on. I told you, you are in the middle of a war, man. Mr. Luas is not who or what he appears to be, you'll see. He killed my family. Anyone with any hint of promise makes him feel threatened. He's an evil, jealous, greedy man, and he will pay for his sins, maybe not today, but some day. Watch your back David. If you don't believe me, you have access to the mainframe. Check the security archives and look up Phil A. Stine. That was my father. They say it was an accident, but I know better. So, I changed my name so I could get close to Mr. Luas, but he's lucky he has you David. Now give me your keys!"

David handed Tony his keys. Tony backed out the door, locking David inside. David heard voices on the other side arguing.

"Why didn't you kill him?"

"He's not a threat," Tony shot back.

"If you don't, I will!"

David heard the sound of gunfire, and ducked instinctively as bullets pelted and penetrated the door. A computer sizzled and popped in protest when struck by a swarm of bullets that had gotten through. The angry voices outside grew more insistent, joined by more voices. Then, as quickly as it began, it stopped.

David fell to the ground, motionless in a pool of his own blood; he was hit. Keys jingled as the door lock clicked open.

The door flew open, and a sweet voice cried out, "David! David, are you okay?"

It was Michal!

"Please God, let him be okay," she pleaded.

But there was no answer. Michal frantically searched for David. She spotted his foot, barely visible from his place of hiding underneath one of the desks.

She ran over and grabbed him, hugging him to her as tight as she could. There was no response. "Lord please, don't do this to me again," she cried.

Michal started CPR and David emitted a quick, dry cough as he finally came to. He had hit his head on the desk when he fell and had lost a lot of blood from his shoulder wound.

"Easy!" David cried, "One of the bullets got through and hit me in my shoulder."

Michal ignored his objections, hugging him all the harder. She was so relieved to find him alive that she could not help herself. "I love you!" she cried.

"Okay, okay, enough of that," Jonathan broke in, "let's get this hero patched up."

A startled David looked from Michal to Jonathan, not sure which surprised him most. Her sudden declaration of love, or the gun he saw Jonathan tucking away.

Luas Corp's personal security and emergency crew came in to secure the area and hurriedly bandaged David's shoulder. David was surprised to see that there were no official police, EMTs, or first responders, just Luas Corp's people. Afterwards, David, Michal, and Jonathan walked out of the building together. As they were leaving, Jonathan and Michal walked ahead as David went over to his vehicle and looked down and saw his keys, the pearl handled snub nose .38, and a small pool of blood on the ground, slightly underneath his vehicle. David was full of questions as he quickly picked up his keys and the gun that Tony had shoved into his face, but David remained silent.

Jonathan turned around and finally spoke up, "I think its time for a Luas family vacation. What do you say David, summer in Bermuda and the Caribbean?"

"Uh, sure," David replied. He gave Michal a little wink, and she smiled back at him, then the three of them made their way back to Luas Corp together. David was relieved that this day had finally ended, but in the back of his mind, he knew Pandora's Box had just been opened and he could not shake an odd feeling of apprehension behind the question that now suddenly haunted him — 'What's next?'